The Three Day Journey

by Dave King

Contents

Chapter 1 - Ready in One 3

Chapter 2 - Check This Out 13

Chapter 3 - Someone's in Trouble 18

Chapter 4 - Hello? 36

Chapter 5 - Did I Do This? 50

Chapter 6 - We May Have Another Problem… 57

Chapter 7 - I Wasn't Planning On That 65

Chapter 8 - Where Are We? 73

Chapter 9 - Appropriate Measures? 88

Chapter 10 - A Flood of Memories 92

Chapter 11 - Chou Do Fu 101

Chapter 12 - Who Are You? 110

Chapter 13 - An Offer He Simply Could Not Refuse 116

Chapter 14 - Wen Zhang Sat and Waited 123

Chapter 15 - Apathy and Soundproof Glass 131

Chapter 16 - A Near-Death Experience 138

Chapter 17 - Do You Not Know? 144

Chapter 18 - Road Trip 150

Chapter 19 - Who Would Have Been Calling from Taiwan? 157

Chapter 20 - Where's My Watch? 166

Chapter 21 - Conclusion? 172

Chapter 1
Ready in One

"Thirty years old? Is it really true?" he thought to himself as he sat staring at the wall of his office. He shuffled through a stack of letters, adverts, bills, and invoices, entering a couple of dates and amounts due into his task list. He had reached the middle of the month bill crunch, just prior to taxes being withdrawn from his account, and finances were really tight.

"Ready in one" popped up on the computer monitor as a typewriter sound clicked from the speakers. Half-dazed and nearly asleep in his midday stupor, he pointed and clicked the mouse several times, finally bringing up the digital x-ray of the waiting patient's offending tooth.

The image clearly illustrated the reason for the dental visit, and Dr. Campbell hopped up from his modest chair and headed out to the operatory one.

———

Yi Cheng listened intently as the real estate agent chattered on and on about the price of the land and buildings and the seller's willingness to negotiate a fair and reasonable figure. Yi Cheng was only there by chance.

He had met the agent at an English class three weeks prior and had come hoping to offer some tutoring in his now well-studied English in exchange for a bit of an apprenticeship.

"Deng yi xia, deng yi xia! Hold on one moment," interrupted the investor as his da ge da (cell phone) chimed a decidedly low-tech sounding version of the latest Britney hit. "Wei?" he questioned as he stepped away and began a conversation so loud and full of expletives that Yi Cheng had to turn and walk the other way to avoid the ongoing and increasing throbbing that was all too frequent nowadays from his past cycling accident.

He stepped out of the main building on the lot and looked up at the sheer magnitude of the three twenty-three-story buildings. Yi Cheng was grateful for the interruption, as he had grown weary of the agent's conversation and overwhelmingly aggressive personality. He put his hand in his pocket and found the mostly empty pack of cigarettes and the lighter. Lighting a cigarette, he watched the smoke diffuse into the air over the busy street corner and thought of the mission he had been on so many years ago. "I didn't used to smoke," he thought.

———

Washing his hands, he stuck his head into the operatory and ventured a glance at the monitor just behind the patient's head. His eyes settled on the little red cross indicating a latex allergy, then drifted to the upper left corner of the screen where it read: "Aaron Rockwood, 34."

"So, Aaron, what's going on with that tooth?"

"Well," he replied, "This tooth has been killing me since last Tuesday! I had some sensitivity at first, but now I can't even touch it without jumping out of my skin. I took some ibuprofen 800s from something in the past, but for the past couple of days, I haven't been able to sleep or concentrate at all. What do you think is going on?"

He shared that he was sorry to be the bearer of bad news but thought that the tooth was going to need a root canal. Dr. Campbell was certain from the symptoms and the textbook X-ray that this tooth needed some serious and aggressive treatment. As Dr. Weber used to say, "Endo or out-o," meaning that to solve the problem facing the patient and himself, there were only two options. The first and most desirable (assuming the tooth was otherwise salvageable) was a root canal. The second option was to extract the tooth.

They discussed the options, the pros and cons, and the long-term repercussions for a moment and finally came to a meeting of minds. As he proceeded with the injection, inserting the 27-gauge needle just medial to the pterygomandibular raphe, slightly superior to the height of the mandibular occlusal plane, his mind was suddenly filled with images of the Taiwanese night market. He could hear the sounds of the people around him and smell the flavors of the many foods and treats served to the interested passersby and the hungry alike.

He withdrew the needle and recapped it, carefully scooping up the cap to avoid another painful and embarrassing needle stick. He excused himself to let the anesthetic set in and meandered back to the modest chair in his private office. There, he plopped down on the cushion just hard enough to cause a "fsssssshhhhhh" sound that generated a much-needed chuckle.

He gazed past his monitor to the pictures taped to the back of the computer credenza, which displayed the artwork of two of his three little girls.

His oldest daughter had drawn a little heart and colored it in with a stripey pattern. Below, she had written "I LEO YOU," which was her way of spelling "I love you." He thought about how much he loved spending time with the kids and how cute they were. He chose not to dwell on the stress and agitation they sometimes generated in his life. Instead, he chose to think about other things.

He entered a few comments into the patient's chart, provided an interpretation of the X-ray, and recapped the treatment discussion before stepping out to begin the task of extirpating the pulp of Aaron's tooth.

―――――

Yi Cheng had finished his cigarette, sent a quick email to John, and contemplated the meaning of the universe for just a few minutes before moving back into the building to engage in some sales talk of his own.

―――――

Wen Zhang studied the crack that had suddenly appeared, sprawling across the floor. He pulled out his cell phone and snapped a photograph, quickly emailing it to himself. As he crossed the length of the room, memories of a certain collapsed shopping center in Korea flooded his mind, which had claimed the lives of hundreds of people. The architects and engineers should be notified, and the public should be alerted. No matter how crooked his boss was, lives were at stake, and many were children.

He fast-stepped across the basement storage room of sub-level 6 and slid quietly through the service door adjacent to the frozen foods section of this posh underground grocery store. "I'm sick of it," he thought, biting into the leaf-wrapped betel nut. 'I've covered for him enough, and I'm done."

He climbed into the elevator and watched the doors slowly close. His mind wandered back to the time he had spent in the Middle East working for the shipping company. He was nearly a king there, although comparatively speaking, a millionaire among billionaires is still nearly penniless. The assignment had come shortly after he had cleaned his life up and tried to make amends with his distraught and untrusting ex-wife. He was nearly overwhelmed by depression when his wife refused to allow him to visit his children. At first, there was anger and rage, but he had become somewhat accustomed to controlling his natural human responses. So, he focused and meditated, eventually realizing that his past was too painful to bear, his ex-wife was completely out of her mind, and that he would simply avoid any thoughts of his past life.

He had then decided that his only goal in life should be to accumulate wealth, and he set his sights on amassing a fortune worthy of his ego and pride. His younger life had been spent in selfish pursuits, at times devoid of conscience and ethics, so he had little reservation about returning to that frame of mind.

The elevator eased to a halt, and the doors quickly popped open. The attendant motioned to Wen Zhang, and he exited to the administrative level of the shopping center. "He's dragged me from problem to problem," he cursed under his breath. "I've always been his clean-up man, and all I've got is an ulcer and two ruined marriages, not to mention a host of problems from alcohol and drug abuse."

He headed into his office, pulled his chair out of the way, and opened the outer door to the safe that kept it hidden. He entered the 13-digit combination, inserted the laser-cut key, and turned it, gratified to hear the satisfying "schtung" as the locking steel bars released their grasp on the door, which swung free with an audible creak.

He accessed his email and printed two copies of the photograph he had just taken. After taking the photo off of the printer and verifying the quality, he slid it under the stack of cash he had in the safe, placing the other copy folded in his inner breast pocket. Among other things, this safe contained his insurance policy. It included a list and various supporting documents of all of the shady and unethical dealings of his boss, not partner, but boss, Robert Liu. Although he was directly involved in nearly every minute aspect of every business undertaking, including the underhanded and deceitful endeavors, he had been careful to keep himself out of sight and away from paperwork for anything even slightly unethical. Over the years, he had grown to hate Robert. This was the hatred fed and nourished by constant aggravation and incessant backbiting. Robert had been the downfall of his second marriage. He had discovered them in the office, alone together, and Wen Zhang had nearly attempted to kill them both, consumed by the rage that had steadily built over the years. He had managed to control himself just enough to slam the door as hard as he possibly could, breaking it off its hinges.

The small payout had been no more than a slap in the face, but the pain and embarrassment were terrible in every way. After the long, arduous task of bringing his life around from substance abuse of the worst kind, this was just the payback he was looking for. She had become everything to him, everything that his first wife had been: supportive, loving, concerned, and appreciative. He had nearly broken down his defenses and allowed her to see who he really was, but then he discovered that she was worse than he had ever been. She was only with him for the lifestyle, the money, and seemingly the boss. Robert was going to pay. And it would hurt. He closed, locked, and hid the safe, replacing the key that was around his neck, and headed down the hall to the elevator.

Weaving in and out of the jewelry counters and the many browsing customers on the main level of the shopping mall, his gaze settled on various people as he moved through the large open floor. He saw a tall, thin woman looking at a handbag, an average man trying on watches, and an observant foreigner. They made eye contact as if the white man had been watching him and then, realizing he had been caught, quickly turned away. "This was not your average foreigner," he thought to himself as he flipped open his cell phone and began dialing. Why would an American spy be in the mall, this mall he managed? His phone chimed as the line connected. "Shenma shi?" the person on the other end queried.

Dismissing the misplaced man, he spoke just above a whisper, "Women, you yige da wenti"—"We have a big problem." As Wen Zhang walked through the airlock and out of the building, the foreigner turned, dropped the nondescript item he had been pretending to look at, and nimbly pursued.

―――――

The owner of the building, Robert Liu, had been eagerly awaiting a call from his property manager. He had canceled his plans for an evening out with his investor friends and was now sitting impatiently in his well-decorated private home office. His wife was out with friends, leaving him with nothing to do but sit and wait for the call. The day before, one of his clients, who leased the entirety of sub-level 5 in building 2, had complained of a loud cracking sound followed by a small earthquake-like tremor. No other tenants had reported such an issue. Only himself, the tenant who called, and his right-hand man, Wen Zhang, knew what had happened.

It took every ounce of Robert's self-control to resist the urge to pull out every hair on his head. Not now. Not when I'm so close. For so long, Robert had been planning to sell the buildings. He wanted to retire to Montenegro and live the remainder of his life enjoying the lake and the lifestyle that comes with extreme wealth. He was selling the mall, and had a couple of huge corporations and investment firms looking into the acquisition. There was also one smaller corporation owned by a local Taiwanese investor that claimed to have the millions to purchase the property, but Robert wasn't fooled.

He really had a golden egg with this property. One of his largest under-the-table deals had been to blackmail the builder of the mall into accepting an astronomically low bid. This was, of course, in response to some persuasion of the photographic type. Wen Zhang had a photo of the builder in a compromising situation that would devastate not only his family life but also his professional life. The deal was struck, and the buildings were built. Now, all Robert had to do was offer a modest price, and he was sure to make a huge margin of profit, enough to live the rest of his selfish and indulgent life fabulously rich. All that he needed now was some sort of nightmarish report of a foundational problem to give him a coronary.

The sudden sound of the phone nearly caused a coronary. He stood up from his chair and answered the phone, speaking loudly, "Shenma shi?"

Chapter 2
Check This Out

Finishing the last part of the root canal, Dr. Campbell cured the resin filling and removed the rubber dam and clamp. He checked the bite and made a couple of necessary adjustments before excusing himself and asking the assistant to take a quick postoperative X-ray of the tooth. The assistant began to discuss post-op instructions and a prescription with the patient. Meandering back to his office, he once again made a note in the chart regarding a measurement or procedural detail. His gaze drifted to the drawing his daughter had made, positioned to the left of his computer. Just then, his Blackberry chimed.

An email from his old friend Yi Cheng, who lives halfway across the world, just arrived. Last week, he had managed to track down his old friend through some enhanced search engine functionality and had begun to reestablish ties to the island he had grown to love so much.

The email was short, but it gave Dr. Campbell the impression that Yi Cheng had been doing a lot of nothing lately. He mentioned that he had been shadowing a real estate agent around and had begun to take an interest in the real estate market.

"That was it, of course. Another short email, just enough to justify the new electronic toy," he thought.

―――――

Yi Cheng followed the agent and the interested investor into the elevator and then down the series of escalators into the market. He hated the American-style market, full of pre-packaged, pre-processed, and pre-plastic-wrapped foods. It was, however, the anchor of the mall and had always drawn in a constant stream of customers. While the upper levels were always changing vendors and rearranging locations, the grocery store remained the same.

The tour of the mall had taken them over 2 hours so far, and Yi Cheng was worn out and in desperate need of a smoke. He asked one of the clerks where the restroom was and headed off as soon as the investor picked up his cell phone, again screaming obscenities through the phone to some unlucky administrative assistant. Yi Cheng missed the turn while digging for his lighter and ended up in a storage room with just a few boxes haphazardly strewn about the large, gaping space. There were a handful of huge columns in the room, bringing the words "load-bearing" to mind. He wandered to the far end and lit up a smoke, hoping the smell and the smoke would draw no attention. As he sat, juggling his cigarette and clicking away at his Blackberry, he noticed what appeared to be a significant crack in the concrete floor of the room he was in. He chuckled and then ignored it, lost in the world of instant emailing. After sending the email, he dropped his half-smoked cigarette on the floor. Stepping on the little tube of rolled carcinogens, a thought occurred to him: "Rebar? Was there no rebar in the concrete?"

He walked back over to the crack and peered down into the darkness. Using his Blackberry as a makeshift flashlight, he estimated the crack to be about three feet deep with an opening of approximately eight inches. It spread from one wall to the other just at the point where four of the massive columns rested on the floor, then climbed up the walls to the ceiling, resembling the lifeline of a deep underground cave. As the crack ascended up the walls, it became less and less of a gaping chasm and more of a simple fissure in the foundation. Clearly, there was no rebar in the concrete. He clicked off four or five photos of the crack and sent them to his American friend with the subject line "Check this out."

As he climbed into his little Honda Fit, the dentist was once again interrupted by the chime of a new email. He lifted the BlackBerry out of his pocket and saw the subject line "Check this out." Ignoring the email for the time being, he headed to the bank to deposit the day's winnings. He had been struggling for some time now; his fledgling corporation barely made enough to pay the bills, let alone give him any paycheck that was worthy to write home about. He had incurred some debts that were far from beneficial and was losing more and more hair and more and more sleep to predatory anxiety. Heading home, he planned to catch the latest American Idol episode on TV and drown his sorrows in a tall, nice glass of Diet Coke.

They had made a huge profit in the last 6 years, profits associated mostly with large numbers of clients and overinflated leasing rates. The location of the supermall was as good as it gets, and the marketing campaign was a phenomenal success. From the very start, the vendors had paid anything Robert and Wen Zhang had asked just to get a spot at the new Zhong You mall. They had been slightly over budget when Robert embezzled from himself to purchase the Montenegro estate. This led to a series of forced poor decisions and blackmailed contractors to keep the project on track. One decision, it seemed, would be enough to ruin his life forever. Wen Zhang had called 5 minutes ago and told Robert of the crack and foundational damage. He wanted to meet personally to discuss a proposition regarding the problem.

Wen Zhang was an irritable man with an all-seeing eye. It seemed like nothing would ever get by him. When Robert took advantage of the construction company by forcing them to work at a reduced cost, it was Wen Zhang who made all of the arrangements. It was Wen Zhang who had caught the President of Bai Hua Construction in a compromising position and had evidence to prove it. It was Wen Zhang who made the arrangements for the price break in the construction budget. But despite all of this, Robert saw all of the profits. He had made the millions, and no one but Wen Zhang knew.

He had been tempted many times to retire the old man, but Wen Zhang knew so many of his dark secrets that he didn't dare go through with the firing. Robert thought gratefully that he had never been the type to blackmail or extort him for all he was worth. And there was plenty to go around, both dark secrets and net worth.

Donning his cashmere coat and snatching up the keys to his Mercedes Benz, he took his private elevator down from the 5th floor of his mansion to the garage level, where he climbed into his M500 and pulled out of the driveway to make the 45-minute trek into the heart of Taichung City. He had a small handgun that he kept in his glove box just for personal protection. He had some training when he was in the military during his 2-year stint, but it had been 40 years since he had fired any weapon. Robert's wife hated guns and with good reason. While waiting at a packed and overflowing stoplight, he slid the compact 9mm handgun into his inner jacket pocket.

Chapter 3
Someone's in Trouble

He arrived at the bank and placed the envelope carrying the deposit into a plastic carrier, sending it off into the digital numerical abyss of the banking world. The red flashing LED on his Blackberry drew his attention again to the email he had received a few minutes prior from his Taiwanese friend, who seemed to have entirely too much time on his hands. He clicked the email open, read the subject line, and studied the miniaturized photos of some sort of crack.

"Well, that's interesting," he thought, then typed into the email gadget, "Someone's in trouble!" and off the email went.

———

Yi Cheng rejoined the other two and briefly inquired about the location of the building's administrative offices. He promptly excused himself from the surprised duo and headed up to the 23rd floor. As he entered the elevator and it began to ascend into the upper reaches of the building, he could see why the administrative offices were located in this building and at this height. The elevator was almost entirely glass on the back side, and the elevator shaft was also almost entirely glass (aside from the steel struts and I-beams), providing the most beautiful view over the city. He could see the Mei Shu Guan (performing arts center) completely surrounded by trees and immaculate gardens. Lost in his memories, he thought back to an evening about ten years ago when he had been involved in a performance by the BYU Young Ambassadors. It was a wonderful evening of singing and dancing, and he had a first-class seat as an usher.

The attendant interrupted his blissful reminiscing with a polite "Xian sheng?" (Sir?) and motioned to move out of the elevator as they had reached the 23rd floor nearly 30 seconds earlier.

It was late into the evening, and Yi Cheng didn't really think he would be able to find anyone there. What he really wanted was to go home and log on to his favorite online chat room. He wandered around for about 5 minutes before seeing a light on in one of the larger corner offices. He headed toward the light and began to pull up the photos he had taken previously.

———

Robert was astounded at the nightmare unfolding in front of him. He had arrived at the restaurant where Wen Zhang usually had dinner. They met and had their usual business-type dinner, replete with stressful financial conversations and the accompanying meaningless cover chatter. Then, after Wen

Zhang downed his last beer, he headed for the restroom. Both were pretty drunk, and Robert did not handle his alcohol very well at all.

"Why had he wanted to meet over dinner? Why not just meet at the office?" Returning from the restroom, Wen Zhang slid into the booth and let fly a string of obscenities that usually came along with his inebriation. He spoke softly then, as though he was not as drunk as he seemed.

"I want thirty million yuan, or I'm going public with all of the secrets. The building needs foundational repairs, and it must be evacuated to make the necessary repairs. That will not be good for business. I want out, and I want out now. I'll give you 24 hours to get me the money, or I'll release the files—you know, the secret ones that only you and I know exist. I will hand-deliver them to the building commissioner and drop a couple of calls to my friends at the news station on the way." He let out the loudest and most guttural laughing streak, loud enough to embarrass Robert and offend nearly everyone in the restaurant. With that, Wen Zhang stood up and marched slowly and lackadaisically out of the door.

Robert sat in shock and awe, watching the selfish little man exit the restaurant. He felt as though the weight of the world had just descended onto his shoulders, crushing him beneath its burden. A rage unlike any he had ever felt before began to gradually build, starting as anger and then slowly increasing into a juggernaut of hatred and loathing. He stood up and began to pursue Wen Zhang out of the restaurant.

―――――

The American, watching from his obscure vantage point, saw the two Taiwanese men leave the restaurant one after the other. He assumed they were headed back to the buildings where the business transaction was to take place. The funds had been wired into Robert's account, the owner of the property, and now it was just up to him to capture the handoff on video. He had previously set up several cameras in the owner's office to capture this enormous deal. As his handler had informed him, the deal was for 5 million USD for one container transported into the US.

Inside that transport container was most likely some sort of bomb? He wondered why everyone at the agency was so tight-lipped about the entire operation and refused to offer any insights into any of the particulars. His orders were to obtain information; that was it. What kind of organization could come up with 5 million USD to pay for transport into the US? Only some sort of government-backed or privately backed group could come up with that kind of dough.

His thoughts were interrupted as the two men were now quarreling very loudly. Robert had caught up to Wen Zhang and was verbally assaulting him on the corner of one of the busiest streets in Taichung City. Wen Zhang fired back, and soon, they were both yelling loudly, attracting a great amount of attention from passersby. They soon separated, and Robert headed towards the street where his M500 was parked. He climbed inside and slammed the door violently, banging his hands angrily on the steering wheel.

Jamison wondered what could possibly be going on in the mind of this man to interrupt the 5-million-dollar deal that was all but completed. Robert started the ignition and sped off down the street, squealing the tires. Pursuing, Jamison maintained a safe distance and followed the Mercedes SUV deep into town to the red-light district. Robert had come here four times over the last week, and at this stage of the game, nothing surprised Jamison more than seeing Robert fly into a rage, ruining his marriage, jeopardizing the security and privacy of his financial future, and his life for that matter. He had over 20 million dollars in his offshore account, including the newly acquired 5 million, all of which had been verified by Jamison's insider contact at the bank. He owned an enormous mansion at Lake Montenegro, Spain, and had already purchased plane tickets for tomorrow to fly himself there, sans wife.

Following his foray into the red-light district, Robert had come to his senses and realized that he needed to do something about Wen Zhang. He had arrived at the corporate office long before Wen Zhang had and was rifling through the office, searching for the safe he knew was somewhere there. In a terrible rage, he turned the desk over and tore the artwork off the walls. Spotting the cabinet positioned behind the tall desk chair, he let his fury go to work on it. Before long, he had kicked the outer door to pieces and was confronted with the most complicated digital safe he had ever seen. "What is this?" he screamed, having completely lost all control of himself. He kicked it once, but like a well-constructed steel-reinforced, waterproof, and fireproof safe, it did nothing.

He tore all of the drawers out of Wen Zhang's desk, looking for the key, but found no success. His anger had been steadily building, and he was now in a state of complete rage and lack of self-control. In this state, completely lacking any grasp on rationality, he dug the handgun out of his inner pocket and released the safety. Placing the barrel firmly against the digital display of the high-tech safe, he pulled the trigger.

His hand was immediately numb, and a searing heat spread instantly up to his elbow. The explosion emitted from the barrel of the handgun threw Robert's hand back so quickly that his wrist snapped completely backward against his forearm. The handgun flew across the room, and yet again, the safe remained unyielding. Robert had a knack for temper tantrums and a lack of self-control, but lately, he had been much, much worse.

―――

Jamison sat quietly, safely secreted away from the happenings in the corner office, and was becoming more and more completely astounded. This evening had gone from strange to mind-boggling and was turning out to be very, very out of the ordinary. Usually, in his line of work, when men were about to make a deal with the devil, they would get drunk, high, or engage in some other form of lasciviousness to distance themselves from the reality of what they were about to do. It amazed him how easily men would trade their dignity, their worth, their integrity, and their families for money. Robert, it seemed, had lost his mind. Perhaps the strain of 5 million dollars had finally gotten to him.

Just then, the elevator door opened. Wen Zhang slid through the door and toward the office where Robert sat with his broken wrist, cursing and shouting obscenities. Jamison remained safely distant in the service corridor with his trusty laptop, staring in disbelief at the unfolding scene. Several weeks ago, he had placed six micro-cameras in various locations throughout the offices and could now see precisely what was happening in Wen Zhang's office through three of those micro-cameras. There was movement on one of the camera displays that had previously been silent and motionless. Wen Zhang was moving down the main hallway toward the corner office with the light on. His corner office.

Jamison watched, astounded, as Wen Zhang reached into his coat pocket and withdrew a semi-automatic handgun, much like the service model he himself carried. Wen Zhang suddenly became very agile for an old man and flattened himself against a wall.

"Who is that?" thought Wen Zhang. The transaction had been arranged for tomorrow.

Wen Zhang peered around the corner to see Robert sitting on the floor, holding his wrist. The office was a mess, and his private safe looked like someone had tried to blast a hole in it. Robert had not seen him yet, and he wondered if he should just leave. Still, he had the upper hand—he was armed. But Robert didn't need to know that, at least not yet.

"What the hell are you doing in my office, and what the hell are you doing TO my office?" shouted Wen Zhang, trying to feign true uncontrolled rage.

Robert turned, and every ounce of color drained from his face. He said nothing. Standing, he turned to face his longtime employee, who had now turned on him.

"I've had enough of your condescending, imperialistic, big-picture, pigheaded leadership, Robert! You've ruined my life more than once. You took my wife; you took my life and flushed them both down the toilet. I have put some things in motion that will destroy you, and there's really nothing you can do about it."

"Do you really think you could destroy me? What could you possibly do that would destroy me?" He was bluffing, as he knew Wen Zhang had more evidence on him than he himself was even aware of.

"Well, apparently, you are a terrorist, Robert. Did you know that? You've just agreed to provide a mode of transport for a nuclear weapon into the US. Did you know that? This crack-in-the-floor thing is just very interesting timing, especially for you. The real horror of what is going to happen to you should be clearer tomorrow. You didn't think I had it in me, did you? Well, you'll get what you deserve, that I promise you, that I promise you."

Robert stood dumbfounded and in pain. A wave of nausea suddenly swept over him, and the pain in his wrist and forearm threatened to bring him to his knees. He doubled over and vomited on the floor.

"Do you ever read what you sign? I had an assistant place a pile of papers on your desk yesterday, and you signed every single sheet. Must have been in a hurry, as you signed a single transport container from that shipping company you own over to an organization that has strong terrorist ties."

"I am not sure exactly where they plan on sending the bomb, but you should have about 5 million more dollars in some offshore account that you didn't know existed. Oh, you won't have it long, or your freedom, for that matter, or even your life, as I plan to give the CIA a ring to let them know what you've done. They've been snooping around *you* for some time, I'm pretty sure. I've been picking micro-cameras off of nearly everything." Wen Zhang lingered on the "you" as if to rub it in Robert's face for all of the grief he had been caused.

"So, here is what happens: you make a call, wire the money we discussed at the restaurant to my account, and then I get out of your life, and you never see me again. If you are lucky, I will give you some evidence that might corroborate your story to the government who really likes the US CIA. You really don't have many options here anyway. You are the one who signed the papers, you are the one the government will come after, and you are the one whose life will be spent in some cell in Guantanamo Bay as an enemy combatant to the US government. So, what do you say?

Robert doubled over and vomited again on the floor. The booze, the stress, and the pain were finally getting to him.

Wen Zhang felt the hair on the back of his neck stand up in warning and heard footsteps on the marble floor entering the office. His hand slid into his pocket and grasped the firearm.

―――――

Yi Cheng was clicking the thumb keyboard on his Blackberry when he came around the corner. He didn't see two men standing in an office that looked like it had just been trashed or tossed by thieves. He finally looked up just as one of the men turned and suddenly had a gun in his hand, pointing at Yi Cheng's face. Yi Cheng froze... One more click on the keypad of his phone, then it was like slow motion as he felt his blood pressure drop instantly and his consciousness fade. He drifted into a sort of half-life as he felt his head clumsily hit the floor. Suddenly, he became aware that he had felt this way before, just after hitting the pavement following the tragic bike accident that altered his life so profoundly. He could still see just a little bit, but his vision faded so quickly that it was only a haze and a visage of a looming dark shadow.

What happened next was truly incredible.

A bone-rattling crack reverberated through the entirety of the mostly concrete building. Suddenly, the floor shuddered and groaned as though some terrible leviathan caged deep within the bowels of the building had come to terrifying life. As quickly and startlingly as it had begun, it stopped dead in its tracks. The crackling and rattling lasted no more than about 4 seconds before stopping completely. Then, nothing but silence.

Robert stood and looked up at the ceiling, wiping his mouth with his sleeve. The expression on his face conveyed a sense of despair, as if it were the end of the world. Wen Zhang, having had enough of Robert, impulsively squeezed the trigger. The 9mm slug whipped Robert's head back as it entered just under the left eye and lodged somewhere in the grey matter of his brain. Robert fell straight backward like a board and crumpled upon hitting the wall, blood spilling from the wound on his face.

A strange creaking noise began, and then the building started to reverberate and sway slightly. Fire alarms blared from every corner, and water sprayed from the ceiling sprinklers.

Wen Zhang put his hand on his forehead and wiped the water from his eyes. He glanced over at the strangely out-of-place man he had never met, the man who was passed out on his office floor, and asked himself, "Who on earth is this?"

The CIA agent sat motionless, wondering what was happening to the building. He closed the laptop, stuffed it into the backpack, and then started down the stairs of the 23-story building. The cameras were still recording but would probably not catch anything as the sprinklers and the nonstop spray would obscure most of everything.

He would fall back to plan B, assuming that the handoff had not occurred prior to the water and the earthquake. It was very strange that an earthquake happened at exactly the moment he needed to capture the most. With the images and evidences he was to gather, the CIA, in cooperation with the Taiwanese government, would take action against Wen Zhang, Robert, and their connections in terrorism. There had been evidence for some time that Robert had aided some minor terrorist cells in the US, none of which had been able to take any action as yet, thanks to the work of Jamison and other agents like himself. Now, it seemed that Wen Zhang was the mastermind of the whole deal. He was the one who made the calls and the arrangements. "More information," he thought, "I need more information."

As he reached the 18th floor, still in the stairwell, he could hear the screams of the scared people below him. He had been through quite a few earthquakes, but none like this. The earthquakes he was accustomed to always began as mild swaying and perhaps culminated in some sort of moderate shaking and vibration, but never any sort of crack or shuddering.

As he reached the melee of people pushing, fighting, and screaming, he realized that he might never make it out of the building if the earthquake continued.

Wen Zhang wondered what he should do with this man, this unconscious man who had entered in the middle of his wholly ungratifying resignation speech to Robert.

Another huge crackling noise and a monstrous shuddering awoke the leviathan once again. Building two began to give way due to the faulty construction of its crucial underpinning.

Wen Zhang could hear the steel I-beams and inadequately reinforced concrete begin to strain and pop as the immeasurable weight of the middle building began to settle slowly lower into the buckling infrastructure. These tall buildings were not meant to sway, nor were they fitted with any type of earthquake protection in the foundational substructure. They were all connected at two locations by walkways that crossed the 22nd floor and the 11th floor. There was an enormous sign anchored on the 18th floor, bearing the name "Zhong You Bai Huo Gong Si" that spanned the entire width of the three buildings. The sign had come loose from its moorings and began to swing away from the first and second buildings, descending toward the street as the anchors to the third building began to snap and twist.

Again, a huge shudder screamed through the building as the second building slowly broke free of the other two structures and began to lean slightly toward the street. The foundation had not given way completely yet; actually, it seemed like it would hold in that position.

Wen Zhang could see the building beginning to go over. He panicked and, dropping the gun to the floor, tripped over the fallen Yi Cheng. As he righted himself, he noticed a small button-like object attached to the corner of the desk.

"A camera! Another camera!" He immediately popped the camera off the desk corner and walked over to the safe, which was mangled and damaged. Rolling it over, he withdrew his key and opened the back door. He pulled out all of the pertinent paperwork, documents, and most of the cash. Stepping over Yi Cheng, he headed to the service elevator. On his way over, he kicked a small device, then bent over and picked up the BlackBerry, dropping it into his pocket.

He turned to Robert, wiped the gun he had used to assassinate his boss, and placed it in Robert's hand to make it look like suicide, matching the suicide note Wen Zhang would work on that evening.

The service elevator required a key, which Wen Zhang had. His trip down the 23 floors was quick and easy. He exited the building via the back entrance, looked back once to make sure he wasn't followed, and after walking about six blocks away, hailed a taxi. As he stepped into the taxi, the phone he had gleaned from the unconscious and surprised guest began to sing. Wei?

———

Jamison descended three floors and then found the service elevator himself. Pulling out a set of lock picks, he opened the door and activated the elevator to exit the building. He also took the back exit, away from the teeming crowds, and found his moped.

He first buzzed off to a restaurant to see if he was being followed by anyone, a habit he had developed of late, as he thought he may have seen a dark-skinned man previously in several locations he frequented. Satisfied that he was not followed, he went to his upscale hotel room to review the video footage and see if he had obtained the information he needed.

Yi Cheng awoke as the second building toppled completely. The building had gently leaned about 5 degrees toward the street and remained in that position for about 2 hours. During this time, the crowds had plenty of time to exit the buildings, and the police and fire departments had arrived. Surrounding homes and buildings had been evacuated as well. Search and rescue scouting teams had conducted a cursory sweep of the three buildings but had missed the office where Yi Cheng lay unconscious on the floor. Subsequently, the massive supporting columns in the basement and foundation had given way on the opposite side of the building. As a result, it swung back away from the street toward a densely populated but now completely evacuated housing area.

As Yi Cheng awoke, he felt as though warm hands were gently wrapping him in blankets of softly sewn silk fabric. When he regained his ability to comprehend the world around him, he immediately opened his eyes. The image of a man with a gun pointed at him caused a sudden surge of adrenaline, and he gasped. Looking around him, he saw no gun and no one pointing a gun at him.

He tried to stand but was unable to do so. It took him 10 minutes to massage his legs and reestablish the blood flow and neural control that he needed. The cycling accident had been devastating for him, resulting in a brain hemorrhage requiring emergency surgery, a spinal cord injury requiring vertebral fusion surgery, and subsequent complications from both surgeries. One complication was constant problems with his sciatic nerve on the right side. If he sat or lay for too long in the wrong position, he would be unable to use his right leg for as much as 30 minutes.

He stood, looked around, and saw the dead man lying on the floor with the gun in his hand. Yi Cheng fought off a wave of nausea and moved quickly toward the exit. He stopped at the elevator and suddenly realized that he was soaking wet. The whole building was soaking wet. He took the fully functional elevator down to the first floor, where he discovered that he had been the only person within about 5 blocks of the entire mall. Looking to his right toward the open plaza between the buildings, he could see that there was no longer a second building but a huge pile of rubble covering the entirety of the street and plaza. He could barely breathe and felt his lungs beginning to react in their usual asthmatic spasm. He again began to lose consciousness, but this time, he was able to sit slowly and then lie down on the ground. The darkness came, the warmth faded, and all he could feel was the dust in his lungs and the cold marble floor beneath him.

Chapter 4
Hello?

John felt another vibration from his Blackberry and pulled the PDA out of his pocket. This email was distinctly different from the previous emails sent by his friend Yi Cheng. The photo depicted a man pointing a gun at the camera, standing over some sort of slumped figure.

John's first impression was that YI Cheng had been at a movie and had sent a picture of the film to him through his camera phone. He stared at it for a moment, then dismissed it as unlikely.

He drove home and was nearly there when he pulled the picture back up while at a stoplight. This time, he used the zoom feature to check for pixelation and any edges on the screen of the movie he was watching. There were none; it looked like a legitimate photograph. He decided to call his friend back and ask where he had found the image. It was a good justification for paying the nearly $3 per minute of international cellular rates he would incur. Scrolling down to the phone number inserted in the signature of the email, John added the international dialing prefix and the country code for Taiwan and then waited for an answer. After about 10 seconds of clicking and securing the trans-Pacific phone line, he heard the distinct ringing. With a click, the phone line connected, and there was a brief silence before the customary Taiwanese answer: "Wei?"

The caller responded with a familiar Chinese greeting. In Mandarin Chinese, John spoke: "Hey, it's John. Remember me? The one you've sent nine million emails to today?" Silence followed. "Hello?" he repeated, this time in English, then again in Chinese: "What was that picture of, or was it just another joke like the crack in the floor?"

―――――

Wen Zhang sat in the taxi, surprised by the English-accented Chinese coming from the other end of the line. He had seen the name come up on the caller ID, along with a picture of a young, thin white guy. Deciding to play it off as a wrong number, he began to speak in Taiwanese. He said a few things like, "This is not the right number, and I think you misdialed," before hanging up the phone.

"Well, it looks like we have a big problem, don't we?" Wen Zhang thought to himself. "Who is this American, and is he somehow connected to the micro-camera and the man who appeared in the office just moments ago?"

―――――

Staring at the little screen on the phone, John wondered if it was really a joke or not. Yi Cheng had sent him some emails in the past few days and forwarded emails that were pretty corny by American standards but might live up to the standards of Taiwanese humor, but this didn't seem to be humor. There was no punchline, no joke to follow, and no Yi Cheng. He dialed the right number; he knew he did.

He pulled into the driveway of his house and pushed the garage door opener. The garage door opened, and John parked his little sub-compact squarely in the middle of the third parking slot of the garage. It was date night, and the sitter was already there, ready to watch the kids. He hopped up the stairs and through the garage door into the kitchen, greeted by three little girls screaming "Daddy." They then went frolicking off into the nether reaches of the house to hide until they couldn't stand it anymore.

———

Wen Zhang sat down at his computer desk after thoroughly cleaning and showering himself. He wanted no trace of the incident on him. He had to prepare to go off to his new home in Spain, on the lake at Montenegro. Robert was so dense that he had signed the entire stack of papers that Wen Zhang had given him, including the two for the transfer of ownership of the real estate, the one for the creation of the numbered Swiss

~ 38 ~

account, and the three transferring all assets to his business partner. He had immediately had them notarized and photocopied multiple times, followed by secreting away the originals somewhere that no one would ever even begin to think of.

He opened the application interface that allowed him to run background searches on individuals and companies they dealt with, adjusting some settings to grant access to the USA database of persons and businesses. He typed in the name of the caller he had deceived and was gradually inundated with hundreds of possible matches. Entering a phone number to narrow the search, he watched as the hourglass turned. The database gradually filtered the entries until finally yielding its contents: one line, one entry, one name.

He pulled out a drawer in his desk, retrieved the disposable cellular phone he had saved for just the occasion, and dialed a number that only he knew. On the other end of the phone was an individual he never wanted to meet at any point in his life.

These people, he thought, were the most fanatical and hateful individuals he had ever encountered. There was no stopping their hatred; not with guns, bullets, bombs, governments, jobs, security, or otherwise. They had no regard for human life of any persuasion. They only knew hatred. They only sought death, and they only wanted to destroy everything free and democratic.

The line connected. He heard a voice—soothing and gentle, yet strangely deceptive and vindictive. His spine tingled. He spoke the phrase, some passkey, some utterance of ignorant, passive allegiance to this destructive and maniacal movement, under his breath. Then, he listened intently as the phone was slowly handed to another voice. Again, the utterance of allegiance, the promulgation of acquiescent support escaped his lips.

"Who do you think you are?" The voice spoke abrasively, laced with a latent rage. "Did we not arrange to meet on the next day? Why do you trouble me now? Do you not value my life? You should value yours a little more, my friend." He spoke as though he had no interest in displaying or procuring any sense of humanity or normality. He spoke as though his one purpose in life was to aggravate and kill. It did not matter to him why or how, but just to kill and to kill efficiently.

Wen Zhang spoke, "Our position has been compromised; I believe something may have leaked."

———

Jamison sat in his hotel room, reviewing the camera footage repeatedly. He watched as Robert entered the room, rummaged around, located the safe, kicked at it a couple of times, then pulled out a semi-automatic handgun and foolishly attempted to break into the steel safe, resulting in him breaking his own wrist. At that moment, Wen Zhang entered the room with his gun drawn, initiating a conversation filled with threats, insults, and rage. The situation escalated quickly, culminating in murder. Then, something strange occurred: a third man stumbled into the corridor while distracted by his cell phone, only to find himself caught in the confrontation. He looked up, saw the man with the gun pointed at him, and promptly passed out cold on the floor. The murder was surprising, especially considering the deal that had been struck and the money that had changed hands. Afterward, there was nothing but shaking and water from the sprinkler system.

"Had he missed something? What was going on that he had not planned for?" They still had no way of tracing the exact connection back to the terrorists, but Jamison knew there were disposable cellular phones in use, likely many of them forming a network of untraceable calls.

He had bugged Wen Zhang's apartment several times and placed various cameras in different locations around the apartment, but none of them had worked. They all failed. The only possibilities were that Wen Zhang was using a very high-tech device to eliminate any broadcasting out or into the building he lived in, he was in the wrong apartment, or he was very adept at finding hidden spy equipment.

Jamison decided it was time to conduct a shakedown of the apartment to search for the cell phone and cameras and to glean more information about the terrorist cell that had infiltrated the business world of Robert and Wen Zhang.

He loaded his backpack with all the high-tech gear he could stuff into it, then hopped on his moped and sped over to an apartment complex about 3 miles away. As he negotiated the ultra-dense traffic, a thought occurred to him: "I wonder if Wen Zhang has any security in place?"

He parked his motorcycle three blocks away and walked quickly through this market section of town, weaving in and out of the motorcycles parked in various positions across the sidewalk. He stopped for a few minutes at a small store, where he made a random purchase of guava nectar. He had done this countless times so that he could, in a non-direct way, check and look out to see if someone was following him.

This little shop was one of many where the front room of a home had been converted to allow for retail sales of varying persuasions. After the guava nectar, he slipped out the front door and continued wandering purposefully through the crowded streets.

He arrived at the apartment complex and waited in the nearby shadows until one of the many residents either came or went, opening the outside monitored security door. He jogged up to the front door just as he saw someone exiting the building. Carrying on a rather convincing conversation about his day at work on his cell phone, he dug into his pockets for his keys. As the door popped open, he held it for the exiting resident, who paid him little heed as he crept in and passed the security guard stationed at the far end of the lobby. He moved toward the elevator shaft and pressed the up button. As he waited for the door to open, he continued his conversation with his cell phone, speaking entirely in Mandarin Chinese to avoid drawing any undue attention to himself. Entering the elevator, he began the quick ascent to the 73rd floor—the penthouse. Wen Zhang lived on the penthouse level, enjoying a beautiful view of the smog-enshrouded city and the mountains to the east. On a clear day, Jamison imagined looking to the west and perhaps seeing the strait of Taiwan, with the body of mainland China distantly beyond.

He took the elevator to the 71st floor and then pressed the button for the 33rd floor as he exited.

He walked to the back of the building to the service elevator, where he ascended one more floor to the 72nd floor. There, he located the main heat and electrical chase and lifted the hinged service door to climb in. As he opened the steel cover, he heard a click and a wsssshhhh. His backpack jumped as the bullet embedded itself into some outrageously expensive electronic component. Surprised, Jamison dropped into the heat chase and pulled the cover over him. "How was he followed?" he thought. "Who could have possibly known he was coming?" He had doubled back three or four times to make sure he was not followed. "This must be some personal guard of Wen Zhang. Some gun for hire, with a mark on Jamison," he thought to himself.

He maneuvered up the shaft of pipes and heating vents to the 73rd-floor service door, located just outside the back door of the apartment. This back door was only approachable by the emergency exit stairs and the heat chase. Most likely, he would not go undetected, so he prepared himself for the onslaught. He withdrew his handgun and screwed the silencer into the barrel. To his surprise, there was no one there to greet him. "Had there only been one guard? Perhaps there was a guard posted at the front door, or was it some sort of trap?"

After listening carefully at the door for more than 5 minutes and sensing no others present, he removed the lock picks from his pocket and began to work on the door. The deadbolt slid open with no sound at all until it latched in the open position, triggering the alarm. Jamison heard the sound of the electronic contacts generating the impulse to sound the alarm and swore under his breath. He withdrew his weapon and stepped back into the shadows away from the door, gun poised and ready. The alarm began to beep slowly at first, waiting for someone to enter a passcode, then more quickly. No one came to the door. Jamison made a snap decision and ran headlong into the apartment, weapon drawn and ready to fire. He sprinted through the kitchen, the study, and then through the bathroom to the location of the screaming alarm, where he tore the panel from the wall. Quickly, he disconnected the speaker and silenced the alarm. He had only a few minutes before the police arrived, assuming there were no more security personnel present.

Another metallic click and wssshhh put Jamison on the floor. The bullet had embedded itself in the wall just over his left shoulder. His reflexes served him well. He rolled behind the desk and positioned himself to return fire. Looking carefully under the desk, he could barely see the shadows of the soles of the shoes of his attacker standing just behind the door opposite the desk, about 30 feet away. He waited for a lull in the shooting and aimed carefully at the door.

Gently squeezing the trigger, he watched in near-slow motion as the first bullet pierced the door with a loud pop. The door immediately exploded into a shower of splintering wood. Repeatedly squeezing the trigger of the silenced weapon, he blasted a small hole in the door. The third bullet passed completely through the newly formed hole and lodged somewhere in the upper thigh of the other man. The man screamed in surprise and agony and fell to the floor, dropping his weapon in a clumsy rattling of metal. Jamison quickly moved to the door and, in less than 2 seconds, was standing over the crumpled man with his gun raised, eyes darting through the rooms and corridors.

"Ni shi shei? *Who are you?*" asked Jamison. "Where is Wen Zhang?" The man was squeezing his thigh and rocking back and forth as the blood poured from his wound. "I am security," was all he could manage before he lost consciousness from the shock and blood loss. Jamison tied a necktie around the man's leg to stop the bleeding, then proceeded to rummage through the desk of the wealthy businessman, Wen Zhang. Interestingly enough, there was a pile of his very own cameras and spying devices in the second drawer down on the right. He searched the desk again for anything useful, then tore the apartment apart to make it appear like a robbery. As he walked back through the office, he noticed the power button on the computer at the desk flashing. It was in standby mode. "Perhaps," he thought.

He heard banging on the front door as he was powering up the computer. As soon as the screen came up, Jamison snapped several photos and headed out to the balcony. Just missing the newly arrived police force, he managed to locate the lightning cable, that huge 3-inch braided steel cable that channeled any lightning strike electricity from the roof to the ground. Jamison slowly climbed down to the 70th floor, where he broke a window and entered the building again. After negotiating the apartment and its absent residents, he took the elevator down 68 more floors, where he again exited and then slipped down the stairs and out the back door.

Jamison made sure to backtrack and cover his tracks very thoroughly. When he reached his hotel, he proceeded to examine the image he had acquired with his 8-megapixel camera. The image was slightly out of focus, but with a minor adjustment to the clarity of the picture, it became clear.

It was some sort of background-checking software designed for the purpose of digging up any dirt on anyone you could think of. He had several photos of the screen, but with the high-resolution camera and some imaging tools he had, he could read and decipher all of the information he needed.

"Who was this?" he thought. "Was this some contact, some member of the terrorist cell that Jamison had been researching for weeks?"

Jamison had decided that it might be good to have a tail on the dentist from Kansas City, the one who had received the email and the photos. If the terrorists found out what happened and who he was, he would most likely be taken care of quickly. A car and an agent had been dispatched to follow and observe the dentist, making sure to stay out of the way and out of mind. He felt reasonably confident that the dentist would be safe; after all, who doesn't like a dentist? All of the usual precautions had been taken—the phone tapped, the cell phones tapped, and the home and offices bugged. If this guy was in on it, they would know for certain. One phone call, and he had given the new player on the scene his own personal watchdog. Information, they needed information.

―――――

Wen Zhang had spoken with Ramseys for about 4 minutes, providing the needed information about the man who was their mutual problem. He had sent an email to him to provide details, addresses, etc. Ramseys used a code name whenever he spoke with Wen Zhang to maintain anonymity, plus he liked the way it sounded.

John Campbell was a dentist in a suburb of Kansas City, Missouri. He attended Central Missouri State University, the University of Missouri Kansas City, and the University of Missouri Kansas City School of Dentistry. After being in practice for about two years, having started his own practice and accumulating an astronomical amount of debt from school and his business, he struck a vein of gold when he wrote his first mystery/action novel.

This man was married with four children, a mortgage, two cars, and a bunch of families in the area. He seemed a bit under suspicion, not quite the type of person Wen Zhang or Ramseys would have suspected as a CIA informant or agent. Nevertheless, the order had been given; the hit would take place in the next 24 hours to minimize the possibility that he would meet with his CIA handler and pass on any information that could bring the momentous plan to its knees.

Wen Zhang didn't think twice about the prospect that this man was going to die. He was mostly numb to emotion these days. Dr. Campbell would not live out the night. He left the computer on and took the elevator down from his 73rd-floor apartment to the waiting limousine. It was mahjong night, and he didn't want to miss one minute of the fun. As he rode in the limousine, he phoned his shipping supervisor and made arrangements to have the container shipment placed in the basement for his inspection. He would then wait until the terrorists had their chance to insert their goods. Then, he would arrange shipment to the USA. "Pretty simple," he thought to himself. Little did he know that his luck was about to change.

Chapter 5
Did I Do This?

Dr. Campbell had noticed for the past few hours that someone had been trailing him. A nondescript white sedan remained parked outside the dental office and followed him to the bank, then to the fast food restaurant. He played the fool to make the pursuer think he had no idea and had even gone so far as to snap a couple of photos with his camera phone as he pulled through the drive-through. Something was not right; something was wrong. The driver was probably a white guy but kept pretty far back. Dr. Campbell would probably not have noticed him, but with the positioning of the rearview mirror in the center of the windshield, he had no choice but to see everything that was going on behind him.

After picking up dinner, he decided it was time to lose this guy. He shifted the car into "Sport" mode, enabling him to control the automatic transmission completely with the help of the paddle shifters mounted on the steering wheel—one for upshifting and one for downshifting the transmission. Much more fun, and with a much better response.

He made normal progress toward his destination, home, but then made a sudden breakaway, crossing three lanes of traffic and turning immediately down a side street. He had completely blown the pursuing CIA agent out of the water. Jamison's watchdog had no choice but to make an illegal U-turn and attempt to pursue the much more nimble Honda Fit.

John had positioned the car in a driveway slightly behind another car so that he could see the trailing car pass by him unnoticed. The agent blew by his hiding place without even a second glance.

"Interesting," the officer thought, "this kid must know that something big is going down. He got pretty spooked. Only the guilty react that way to a pursuit... Very interesting..." Picking up his cell, he dialed Jamison on the other side of the world.

―――――

He had not mentioned anything to his wife, nothing to anyone, really, but had sent another email to Yi Cheng to make sure it had nothing to do with him. No reply. They finished dinner and then sat down to have a Family Home Evening. The kids were very restless this evening, full of energy. Par for the course. "If only I had that energy," he thought. "I could do so much more."

John had just finished putting the kids to bed upstairs in their rooms and had plopped down on the couch to watch some mind-numbing television. He fell asleep on the couch, worn out and exhausted from the day of dealing with non-paying dental patients. He didn't understand why someone would go to Walmart or Target or a car dealership and expect to leave without paying for their purchased goods. No, absolutely not. People pay when they place value on what is important. His irritating dream came to an end as the cat gently padded across his stomach. Frustrated, he turned off the television and headed to the restroom. The door alarm chimed and spoke the words, "basement door."

Spooked, he immediately held his breath. They didn't usually turn on the alarm at night, but after the incident with the man following him in the car, John wasn't taking any chances. There was a loose screen on the basement door, and John thought that it might have created the movement that could have triggered the alarm chime. It didn't make any sense. He washed his hands, then turned off the alarm and went down to scout out the noise.

John found no one. He headed back up to the restroom and began to wash his face. He toweled off his dripping face and then turned on the alarm, bypassing all of the upstairs motion sensors. Just as he was heading toward the bed, he heard a creaking sound from the kitchen. All the hair on the back of his neck instantly stood at attention. His heart rate increased. His eyes widened.

Having no weapons in the home, except for a hunting bow left over from high school in the basement, he frantically thought of what he could use to defend himself. He took three steps back into the bathroom and hunched down, trying to hear the slightest sound from anywhere. As he did, his hand pressed against the lid to the back of the toilet. It made a distinct but quiet "clink, clink" sound as it moved. He picked it up and raised it over his head in preparation for anything. He heard the creaking of the hardwood floor in the hallway and immediately knew that someone was there, someone unwelcome, someone with an evil purpose. He closed his eyes and began to experience the strangest sensation he had ever felt.

It was as if some part of him, some ethereal or spiritual essence, could sense—or physically see—the whereabouts of this person. After closing his eyes and tilting his head back slightly, he envisioned very clearly the precise location of the other man and could feel every movement he made, every breath, every step. He could see the hand gripping the gun. Amazed at this new sensation, this extension of his awareness, he was lost in thought for just a moment, just a split second, and then reality instantly snapped back into frightening focus. The man was immediately opposite the wall he was leaning against.

He waited, poised at the restroom door, as silent as death with his toilet lid cover elevated. "It was a humorous vision," he thought, "or at least it would be later." He had never been so on edge or so energized as he was at that moment. He waited as quietly as possible, waiting for movement. Slow, shallow breaths. Perhaps the intruder had sensed his presence; perhaps he had stopped moving altogether. Thirty seconds passed. Ninety seconds. Five minutes. John began to feel his energy waning, and his arms began to droop slightly as he waited. Then, in a nanosecond, the shortest discernable length of time he could imagine, he experienced a massive surge of adrenaline. His brain flooded his body with epinephrine. His heart rate shot up, and his arms immediately regained their strength as he saw the gun hover into view. The hand that held it had dark olive skin. It was immediately obvious that the assailant had no idea he was behind the door.

John instantly reacted, without any chance for forethought, and lashed out with more force than he knew he had with the toilet cover. Every muscle in his body suddenly became taut at the same instant, as a second surge of adrenaline brought every neuron and neurovascular bundle to full and complete readiness. He had never felt anything like it before. As his muscles flexed in unison, breaking the dead inertia of the 20-pound porcelain, a small grunt escaped from deep within his throat, giving the assailant just a microsecond of forewarning.

The assassin turned toward the open door just as the thick and heavy porcelain slab slammed savagely into his head. The sound was unnerving. It was the sound of crushing bone and destructive force. Half a second later, the gun fired, some last neuronal impulse sent from the fatally damaged brain. He fell to the floor, unconscious. Dead 30 seconds later.

John was completely and utterly enveloped in the power of the adrenaline that had been released into his bloodstream. He smoothly lifted the handgun, removed the clip, emptied the chamber, and tossed them to the floor 30 feet away. The bullet fired in the melee had whizzed just over his left shoulder and punched a hole through the exterior wall after passing through the shower liner.

Alive and energized, he sensed his frightened wife behind him and had to forcibly restrain the beast that had been unleashed within him. "What was that?" she said, frightened, and suddenly gasped as she saw the crumpled shape on the floor in the hallway. John bent down and checked the pulse of the assailant and found none. His skull was crushed. "Did I do this?" he thought, surprised.

"What happened?" she said, frightened and more scared than before. He told her that he heard something in the basement and knew someone was in the house. The toilet tank cover was the only thing he could grab in time. The man pointed a gun at him, and he hit him as hard as he could. She stepped back and turned to go and check on the three sleeping children, who were amazingly still asleep.

John stood, trying not to shake and tremble from the pure adrenaline that had filled his veins. He picked up the phone and dialed 911. The police arrived within five minutes of the call, the police department being only three blocks away. A series of questions followed, then a multitude of photographs capturing a horrific scene of death and blood splattering all over the floor and walls of the hallway. John had called his wife's mother, and the kids and his wife were quickly whisked off to a safer place.

The watchdog CIA agent sat amazed as the assassin was rolled out on a stretcher. "A dentist," he thought. "How is that possible? The Cell sends an assassin, and a dentist kills him in the dead of night. Apparently, he was not in league with the terrorists."

He picked up his cell phone and dialed the international number.

Chapter 6
We May Have Another Problem...

Yi Cheng woke up in Ren Ai Hospital in downtown Dali City, Taichung County, Taiwan. He had been unconscious for about an hour after collapsing outside the building. Immediately, a nurse came to his bedside and began asking him questions. A series of beeps and alarms drew attention to Yi Cheng, and a number of doctors and auxiliaries rushed to him.

He managed to fight off the onslaught of people wanting to ask him questions after the largest shopping mall in the country had just collapsed with him inside. While unconscious, he had undergone a series of tests and seemed to be in good health, considering his previous health history.

The nurse then shuffled everyone out and away from the exhausted Yi Cheng. She drew the curtains closed and approached the still feeble man. Her countenance suddenly changed as she spoke, "You have seen a bit too much today, haven't you? I think you deserve a nap." Yi Cheng noticed a twinge of surprise and fear in the pit of his stomach, and he hit the panic button in response to this imposter but heard no alarm. He tried to move out of the bed, but his legs had been restrained. The nurse retrieved a syringe of solution from her pocket and inserted it into the IV infuser. Down went the plunger, and into his bloodstream went the liquid.

The feeling was unlike anything Yi Cheng had ever experienced. Initially, it was just a slight tingling, especially in his fingers and toes. He tried to scream, or at least he felt like screaming, but wasn't sure if he did, as he felt pressure on his mouth from her hand. Then, the sensation gradually spread to include his arms and legs. His vision began to change; much of it was distorted and twisted. He had the distinct feeling that he was no longer in his bed but standing, then floating, then flying. His brain was telling him that he was no longer connected to his body. It was surreal. He felt like he was looking down at himself, sick, exhausted, and weak. Then, a surge of intense emotion, unlike any he had ever experienced, took over his mind. Rage and astonishing hatred bled into passion and cold fear. Another surge of intense warmth and the color orange, and he lost consciousness completely.

The nurse dropped the empty syringe into the sharps container and then mumbled under her breath that he had seen too much and should rest. Exiting the room, she ran into a host of camera crews and reporters. Caught completely off guard, she immediately blushed a bright crimson red and hurriedly shuffled off toward the stairwell. The nurse quickly excused herself, but not before another individual noticed her timely exit. Before she was halfway down the second flight of stairs, a dart silently and effortlessly embedded itself in the muscle of her right arm. She instinctively reached up and plucked the tiny missile from her arm. As she examined the dart, she suddenly lost her balance and slid slowly down onto the stairs, her right arm grasping for the handrail. It wouldn't move! Her arm was totally paralyzed, as was the entirety of her right side. Immediately screaming upon hitting the stairs, she rolled twice before stopping at the landing. Someone was there. He rolled her over, and she looked up at him as her vision began to fade.

———

The white-haired man carefully rolled her over and, noticing the look of utter surprise, spoke. "I'm sorry, we haven't been properly introduced. My name is Jamison; what's yours?" Then, she saw only silent blackness.

Jamison had finished the phone call to his contact in the US and then flipped on the news to see what information they had regarding the building collapse. "Amazing," he thought. The entire building down in rubble. As he scanned the various channels for some information about the collapsed mall, he came upon footage of a man exiting the building. It was the man from the office, the third man!

Immediately, he contacted his police contact and discovered the whereabouts of this man, this seemingly unfortunate man. He went to the hospital, poised as a news anchor for CNN news. He had gleaned much information from his news colleagues about the reason for the collapse and some other dirt on the owner and the managing partner of the mall. Then, he had seen the nurse leave.

She had exited, totally unaware and surprised by the waiting media. What gave her away was the uniform. It was just a little too perfect. All of the other nurses had uniforms that were of varying patterns and different colored tops and bottoms. This nurse had an all-white set of scrubs and the wrong pair of shoes. When she came out of the room, she had something in her hand which she clutched tightly upon realizing that she was not alone. Then her mumbling and her blushing and quick exit.

Here, she lay on the landing of the stairwell. He grabbed her PDA, her cell phone, and the extra syringe she had in her pocket. No weapon. He quickly disposed of the dart, then ran up into the fray of reporters to direct them to the fraudulent nurse.

As the crowds of media headed to the stairwell, he walked quickly into the room that was strictly off-limits. He planted three microdot cameras in varying locations, one close enough to pick up all the audio spoken by the doctor and patient. He checked the patient's pulse and other vitals, then reconnected the emergency button and summoned help. As he exited the room toward the stairwell where the rest of his reporter friends were, he set the syringe he had acquired from the now-sleeping nurse on the patient's chest.

He acted like he was a reporter, took some notes and this and that, then exited the hospital, returning to his hotel where he had posed as a wealthy businessman. He examined the phone and PDA, downloading and recording all pertinent information he could find. A few more phone calls would do the trick, then a bit more fieldwork.

His cell phone rang as he was researching the man in the hospital.

"Jamison, you're not going to believe what happened."

"Okay, what are we talking about?"

"He lost me on the highway after work; then he kills a terrorist assassin in the dead of night? Who is this guy?"

"I'm sorry, what was that?" Jamison queried, "Did you say that he killed the hitman?"

"Yes, the police have tried to keep the identity of the man secret, but I was able to squeeze a bit out of our friendly dispatch girl at the station here. The guy enters the house, has a semi-auto handgun and a silencer, and looks like an attempted execution, but the dentist pounds him with the back cover of a toilet. Can you believe that? Hits him in the face with 20 pounds of porcelain. Kills him. Amazing."

"What?" Jamison dropped his jaw. He was sitting, and he was glad. That was amazing. The hit had taken place so very fast, or rather, the attempted hit.

Jamison ended the call with orders to the watchdog to maintain visual contact with the dentist and to follow him everywhere, even if he needed another agent with him at all times to do so. He vowed to acquire some more information.

"What a total nightmare," he thought as the detective questioned him over and over again about the events of the evening. The detective was distinctly overweight and had very poor personal hygiene habits. His scruffy beard was caked with what looked like flaking skin and food particles, and he emitted a strong body odor—definitely not the pleasant kind. The detective repeatedly asked the same question in different ways and with different inflections. It seemed as though he was trying to confuse the dentist into some slip of the tongue, some admission of foul play, or some sort of anti-nationalistic behavior.

John sat and answered the questions patiently, just wanting to collect the shambles his life had become and go to bed. They were sitting in his living room on the couch, and it was now about 2:30 am. The detective finally gave up or perhaps gave in to the sheer fatigue of the early morning hour. He began to stack the photos and notes in his briefcase and wrap up the conversation. Though his demeanor was offensive and his conversation entirely lacking in tact, he seemed very intelligent. He left his card and mentioned that he would probably be calling the next morning to ask a few more questions. It was at that instant that John remembered the email he had received. He pulled out his BlackBerry and showed the detective several emails, the last being the most interesting. They discussed for a few minutes, and then John dozed off mid-sentence.

The detective gently shook his shoulder and asked that he send the messages to him. John forwarded the emails to the detective's email address and then politely showed the detective to the door.

He fell asleep on the couch and did not move until about 8 am.

When he awoke, the sun was breaking through the windows. His left arm was half asleep as he had slept on it most of the morning. He phoned his wife to make sure they were alright, then showered and admired the mess in his house. It was disgusting. There was still blood on the floor, and the walls and the toilet cover had been broken in half. As he was dressing, the phone rang. It was the detective from the evening before. He had looked at the emails and had no interesting information to report, but he would keep John up to date with any new information that came his way.

Just as he hung up the phone, John heard the sound of breaking glass in the basement.

After a moment of silence from below, he swiftly gathered his belongings, zipped his backpack, slipped on his shoes, grabbed the keys, and headed for the door. As he exited, he pressed the "instant" button on the alarm system, activating the intrusion alarm and summoning the police immediately. Pulling the door closed behind him, he disarmed the car alarm and unlocked the front door of his little Honda.

As he left, the man who had been lurking in the basement stumbled upon a photo album while scanning the bookshelf. This album was titled "Taiwan," so he grabbed it and began to flip through the pages, anticipating the need to leave as soon as possible. After turning only 5 or 10 pages, he settled on a picture of the dentist, much younger and thinner, standing next to someone he knew to be a contact person for his organization. This woman had previously been the mayor of Taichung City and was known for corruption and dishonesty. She also had some less-than-savory connections to organizations like the one he was connected to, the Cell.

The second assailant dialed the number and waited for the third ring. "Ramseys," he said, "we may have another problem with this man."

Chapter 7
I Wasn't Planning On That

He sped off, cruising as fast as he felt he could get away with. He headed to the office where he thought he could get a little respite, but as he pulled into the parking lot, he saw the same white sedan, but this time it looked empty.

He entered the office and sat down in his cushy chair for a moment to collect his thoughts. He dug around in his desk drawer for the key to the little safe, where he kept the emergency cash that he had on hand. Not much, but hopefully, he wouldn't need it for long. There it was, parked at the end of the parking lot, the little white sedan.

He immediately left the office and began to drive out of the city toward the airport. His friend in the white sedan did likewise. He thought for sure that if he could just trick the man following him into believing that he got on a plane, he would be home free. His first impression was to try to contact the detective and let him know someone was tailing him, but for some reason, he had a bad feeling about that. As he drove the 25 miles toward the airport, his more sensible side got the best of him, and he began to dig for the business card he had slipped into his wallet.

"Yes, hi, this is John Campbell. I need to speak with Detective Dibbens, please?" He was placed on hold and, in less than 25 seconds, was speaking with the ill-favored detective. He told him of the latest and mentioned that he felt he had been followed and that someone was in his house. The hair on the back of his neck suddenly stood up as he seemed to sense that something was wrong.

He asked the detective to hold while he pulled over to the side of the road. He pulled over into a gas station that was bustling and parked the car. In the 20 seconds it had taken for him to exit and park, he had another flash of insight illuminate his mind.

He asked the detective if he had any information about the emails he had forwarded, and the response was quite interesting. The detective's tone of voice changed ever so slightly, as if he was concentrating on maintaining his current tone, but just the concentration alone was enough to alter the sound and inflections enough for John to detect the detective's deception. Detective Dibbens spoke only meaningless lies at that moment, and it was very clear to John when the lies ended, as the inflections and tone of the timbre all went back to normal.

Lie number one.

Another question: He asked Det. Dibbens if he had any information on his attacker. Again, the similar change in tone and inflection, again lies.

Lie number two.

John told the detective that he was heading out of town for a couple of weeks just so he could relax and get some distance from the attack. As he spoke the word "attack," his thoughts were suddenly stopped as if snagged on a sharp barb from some gleaming trident fish hook.

At that precise moment, when the word "attack" escaped his lips, his astute sense of hearing picked up "CIA" and "near the airport" as if he were tuned in to some ultra-high frequency radio station. It was as if the person who spoke those phrases had been sitting next to him in the car rather than in the background at the police station, but in reality, the words were barely even audible. In all actuality, John thought, the words were probably not audible at all, but he seemed to be in a heightened state of mind and ability ever since the experience he had the night before in the hallway, before the attack.

Once again, an interruption in his thoughts as the detective suddenly suggested that he come into the police department to sign the official report so that they could close the case. The hair on the back of his neck stood up again, a warning flag. Thinking quickly, John mentioned that he already had tickets and that he would call when he got back in town in about a week. "So be it," said the detective, who then hung up.

"Why me?" he thought. "What have I done to get them upset with me?" He walked into the gas station and purchased some chewing gum, soda, and snacks for the long, destination-less trip ahead.

He was not flying to Puerto Vallarta, Mazatlan, or Rome. Unfortunately, he was driving to nowhere.

He just needed to shake this guy off his tail and keep him away from his family. He left the gas station and pulled back onto the freeway.

Driving the remaining 15 miles to the airport, he constantly watched the car that was at a safe distance behind him. The sedan had actually fallen completely out of view several times, and John thought perhaps he had been seeing things. But as he pulled onto the airport drive, there it was, about three cars behind him.

He pulled into the airport parking structure where he drove around and around until he saw the white sedan in the rearview mirror. He parked and walked into the airport carrying his bag.

The trailing CIA agent followed him into the airport and up the escalator to the terminal level.

"I wonder how this will end," he thought as he trailed this mysterious target into the airport structure. The agent had been pondering for some time how this dentist was connected to the terrorist plot and how he had been aware of the assassin in his home.

"I've seen these scenes before," he thought to himself, "this was clearly staged." "No one would ever think of using a toilet seat cover as an actual weapon!" "He must have killed the man, then hit him again with the porcelain in an attempt to cover the killing." He reached for his handgun, securely fastened on his belt. His fingers found the button that held the steel and resin weapon safely in his holster and pulled the strap loose, allowing the gun to slide free.

Observing the subject's brisk pace as he entered the airport, the agent speculated that perhaps he was planning to leave town or even the country. He could have him watched, but a more appropriate course of action was to capture and detain him. He wanted to question him and determine his motives for being involved in terrorism.

―――――

John slipped into a dark corner just behind the escalator, so close to the machinery that drove it that no one could possibly have heard his heavy breathing over the roar and clacking sounds generated by the large machine.

After waiting a few moments, he gingerly poked his head out and around the escalator, catching a glimpse of the man. He looked like a businessman in a suit. "Typical agent," he thought and waited for him to pass completely up the escalator to the main level of the airport.

John waited another five minutes before venturing out of his safe hold in the dark corner of the escalators. As soon as he could muster the willpower, he made a dash for his car. Stopping just prior to his car at the white sedan, he let the air out of two of its tires.

Although he had eluded the pursuing white sedan and its adept driver, John failed to notice the small blinking black box that had been anchored to the underside of the driver's rear wheel well. A constant GPS uplink was active, and John was being actively tracked by someone other than the US CIA.

After driving for eight hours, John began to doze off slightly. He decided to call it quits when he hit the rumble strip twice in as many minutes. Quickly pulling over into a rest stop, he parked the car far from the center of the parking lot and leaned the seat back to rest. Just as his eyes closed, the dream began.

In the dream, he could see the city lights—it didn't look too out of the ordinary. As the plane landed and pulled into the gate, he felt his heart racing. His first impression as he stepped off the plane and onto the walkway was that of a wall of humidity.

He had spent the previous ten weeks in Provo, Utah, at a Missionary Training Center, and in the winter at that, so when he stepped into near 100% humidity at 80 degrees, it was instant sweat.

"Well, I wasn't planning on that," he thought to himself. Heading to the baggage claim was sheer chaos. With his limited understanding of the Chinese language and his fatigue and sheer excitement, he could do very little to think straight. Somehow, he and his 11 traveling companions managed to find their baggage and head toward customs. As the customs line was very long, he attempted to speak with those around him. Aside from the Americans with him, there was no one who could understand his "Ch-English."

His turn for customs came up, and he bravely strode forward, dragging the modest luggage with him. Upon passing through customs, he was directed through a large door and into a massive room that had a sort of chute running down one side of it where the passengers would be visible to anyone waiting to see.

There, he was introduced to the APs, the assistants to the president as they were called. These were two of the more experienced missionaries who had been assigned to welcome, teach, and train the newly arrived missionaries. After the introductions, they quickly herded the new "greenie" missionaries into a large van and off to the central city of the mission. As he was stepping into the van, his thoughts began to blur, and his mind became awash with discomfort and anxiety. He felt as though someone had just nudged him and nudged him hard. Just as the door to the van parked next to him at the rest stop slammed, John awoke.

Chapter 8
Where Are We?

John had been awakened by the door of the van parked next to him. He looked around to make sure he was okay and that no one was onto him. Then, he locked his car and headed to the restroom. He slid four quarters into the soda machine and pulled out a 20-ounce diet Coke, his first of the day.

He found himself somewhere in Kansas, along I-70, at a rest stop. He wanted to get whoever it was as far away from his family as possible, so he had driven all night or at least most of the night. He had a good drive; he loved to drive. For some reason, it was relaxing. All of that commuting to undergraduate and then dental school had made a place in his life for long drives. He enjoyed the hum of the engine, the sound of the wind, and the aloneness wrapped in the secrecy of the night. He loved to be alone in his car, speeding down the freeway, and all alone with his thoughts. It was relaxing.

He got back into his little car and turned the ignition. Immediately, he realized that something was wrong. His senses began to tingle. He realized that there was a smell, an odor that was out of place. His mind began to race, his thoughts churning through his brain like an outboard motor without any water to engage. He reached for the door pull and couldn't find it. He suddenly realized that he was beginning to lose consciousness. His fingers, hands, and arms were no longer of any use to him, and he seemed to be completely aware yet unable and even incontinent. The sunlight, just peering over the trees ahead of him, started to sway as if blown by a strong wind, and the trees themselves became mere smears of brown and green, devoid of any percussive detail. He coughed in a last-ditch attempt to clear his lungs of this awful poison but failed. He drifted in and out of awareness for a few moments.

He gradually descended into a sort of limbo, where there was nothing but blackness. He noticed only shadows of reality, waves of motion in the absence of any light. There was something else, some consciousness thought, but he was unable to identify the presence and was sinking quickly into nothingness.

Giving up on consciousness, he now focused solely on survival. A strong drive, unlike any he had ever known, was keeping him from falling completely into the blackness that dragged and pulled him down. It was something he could not quite grasp, as if it was just out of his reach. He felt like he was a buoy afloat in the sea and that, except for his moorings to the shallows, he would most certainly drift off into the abyss. A memory came to mind, an uncomfortable memory, yet it was his memory; he owned it, and it was part of him.

The memory began as he walked into the university library at Central Missouri State University, where he had spent two years before and after his mission in Taiwan. He often spent two or three hours there, following lunch with friends to catch up on studying. Most of the time, he ended up dozing off and sleeping until his wristwatch alarm woke him just in time to make it to his daily music theory class. He walked into the library and, swiped his student ID card, opened the gate, and headed straight back to the elevator to head up to the third floor. Positioning himself in the far north corner, he set down his backpack, unzipped the large pocket, and withdrew a large textbook, something about American history and democratic principles. He remembered reading for about thirty minutes, dozing off shortly, and then waking. He dog-eared the page he was at and closed the book. Positioning his right arm on the table, he gently rested his head and closed his eyes. The next images were interesting…

The memory continued as he was dreaming while his head was resting on his now mostly asleep right arm. His arm had begun to tingle after about 45 minutes, and his mind realized the discomfort and lack of blood flow and had subsequently forced his eyes to open. His eyes opened, and with the disruption of sleep, some deeply disturbing dream was instantly transformed into a fleeting suggestion of anxiety. Although the dream was a familiar one, a chord of darkness and stress was struck as his eyes opened to behold the light on the third floor of the university library. The discomfort resonated for only a moment as he realized that he could not move. His eyes were wide open, but he could not move at all. Suddenly, he began to feel a deep sense of gravity and a literal sinking feeling. His first reaction was to grab the table and chair he was on to keep from falling into the dark abyss that was pulling him down. He felt like he was being pulled down, pulled down into a hollow shaft leading straight into the center of a black hole. He struggled for a moment, fighting within himself, a struggle deep within his psyche to keep from falling into some void. Then the sound began. It began as a sort of reverberation of an echo of a bell's toll and then slowly grew into the veracious buzz of a fire alarm. Immediately, his worries shifted from the deep sinking feeling to the buzzing that was now so loud that it hurt. As suddenly as it began, his arms were free, and he regained complete control of his faculties. The buzzing sound faded like a puff of smoke in the wind and left little more than an echo of the sound.

Unawares, locked deep within his memories and completely incapacitated by the drug, John was pulled from his car and roughly secured in the nondescript colored panel van that had been parked next to him for the last few minutes. The rest area had only these two vehicles, and they both left in unison, one behind the other.

Jamison began looking through the phone numbers stored in the disposable cell phone. Interestingly enough, there were three numbers. Usually, those who were trained did not leave any information in the cell phones they used. A good break. He compared the numbers in the phone to those that had been used recently and were known hot numbers. No luck. Probably just purchased these numbers.

He began to wonder if this cell was connected in any way to the intel he had received last week regarding the Homeland Security threat.

He made a secured call to his contact. His contact was incommunicado, so booting up his laptop and logging in through several tedious and excessively secure web portals, he input the phone number into the secure uplink into the national database of Homeland Security threats and hit the jackpot. His jaw dropped. This cell phone number was currently being tracked by the agency as part of a level red threat to Homeland Security. His security clearance was insufficient to grant him access to the agency's top-level database. He needed his contact, and he needed to get to him fast.

─────

The flight had lasted about 13 hours from LAX. John had been drugged and flown aboard a large private jet owned by an oil tycoon from the Middle East. They had flown from LA to Hawaii, where they stopped to refuel and take on some more supplies, then on to Taiwan, where the rest of the Cell had set up a home base to plan and execute the operation.

This group of individuals was a diverse and multinational group. An evolved group of terrorists, one might say. They had been drawn together by a common cause and a mutual hatred of all things capitalist and all things American. Each had their own reasons to be part of this secretive, dark, and terrible organization, but the money offered by the wealthy benefactor was certainly also a nice incentive.

The stronghold had been in the city of Taichung, Taiwan, where many groups had met in the long past. The city was so large and so sprawling that it would be difficult for anyone without immediate membership in the group, intricate knowledge of the city, and an understanding of the language to locate the complex. They had chosen an isolated apartment complex in the suburb of Dali as their headquarters. It was a rather nice building, considering some of the surrounding properties, and also offered a great deal of privacy from the inhabitants that surrounded them. The cell had rented nearly half of the building, some 12 apartments, to provide extra storage space and allow for guests, such as the one they were expecting today.

From the international airport, it took about 4 hours by car to reach the city of Taichung. The Gao Su Gong Lu freeway was still under construction, so most of the highway was only two lanes, one in each direction. This allowed for pretty slow-moving vehicles and long, irritating bottlenecks. The active construction zones on the highway were manned largely by Philippine nationals who had come to Taiwan seeking only a job. Although the pay was meager compared to even poverty standards, to the Philippines, the salary was nearly a dream. They were recruited in droves by some unscrupulous employment agencies who forced them to sign contracts for as long as three years, committing them to slavery in various less-than-desirable occupational settings. Many would come to realize that the employment agencies promised much and delivered little, and would desert, forfeiting their salary, which was paid each quarter or longer. It was a truly unfortunate and manipulative system designed with only one thing in mind: money. Those who ran the system offered so much to the destitute and dirt poor indigent citizens of the Philippines, and yet when the time came to own up to their promises, many of the "bosses" would hold back a portion of the workers' salary as payment of travel expenses or protection expenses, or just as an act of power and cruelty. The men would receive only a fraction of the agreed-upon salary, only enough to barely subsist in Taiwan, let alone save any money to send home to their wives and children. Many of these workers had several children, and leaving their wives and children to come to work in hopes of saving and getting ahead was no small task.

Oftentimes, the men would be lured into the use of alcohol to dull the pain, with illicit drugs to block out the sheer magnitude of poverty and strife. Many were drawn in by prostitutes, a destructive force much more powerful than drugs or alcohol. The travesty and tragedy of prostitution and the sex industry destroy everyone involved; the man is destroyed from the very center of his soul, and the often-trafficked women are repeatedly devalued and abused in a terrible and heinous way. Much of the sex industry revolves around a sense of machismo, pride, and arrogance, and these men kept far from their families and wives with so little affection and enjoyment in life would often turn to those hollow and deceptive torments that so many purvey as pleasure.

Once the party entered the city, the street system was anything but easily navigated and direct. Taiwan had enjoyed a technological and economic explosion in the 70s and 80s and had grown so fast in population and sprawl that little civil engineering had time to be completed. Roads consisted of space between homes, shops, and apartment complexes. You could drive anywhere your car could fit. Fortunately, there was plenty of asphalt to take care of the paving, but in some places, the roads were nowhere near flat.

As the SUV pulled into the parking garage, entering the street-level entrance, the steel door slid up and open, allowing passage into the secured basement structure.

The Taiwanese were very into security. Every home had bars on the windows and doors, and every business was the same. Any older member of society would tell you that it didn't used to be like this. There was a time when the people of the country were open and available to everyone. Much had changed in the past 30 years, much to the chagrin of many. Privacy and security now trumped any sense of community and trampled the front porch communities that had been a mark of the society's pride and openness.

Just as the vehicle was pulling down into the parking garage, the prisoner began to awaken. The drugs had begun to wear off ever so slowly. At first, it was a simple awareness of identity and personal existence. A sort of "I think, therefore I am" moment. After a few moments of struggling with what was happening, a spark lit in his mind, a memory of the drive, the car, and the van. Then, back into another dream. He dreamed so restlessly of the world around him. Smells, sights, sounds, feelings, and thoughts. But it was so much more than dreaming; it was remembering. Although he was unconscious, the sounds and smells were still processed by the sensory systems in his brain and began triggering chemical reactions that ignited many interesting fires of recollection.

He had the most vivid memories, mostly images of different places and people, all triggered by the smells and sounds he was subconsciously aware of: He was sitting at the small round plastic table of the café looking at the bowl of soup and the plate of rice and vegetables. The Taiwanese woman behind the counter was cooking something that smelled wonderful. He could see the shadows of the chopsticks he held in his right hand and feel the coarseness of the bamboo. The traffic, consisting of motorcycles and small autos, continuously flitted by creating a drone, a sound that never left him alone as he sat there on his plastic chair. The memory was so vivid, so all-encompassing, that he could even feel the texture of the cloth of the slacks he wore as the fabric rubbed on his knees. There was a mugginess in the air that made him sweat and a cloud of smoke that was mostly invisible and ever-present that gave him such stains on his white shirts' collars.

He was jarred back into reality as the van door slid open. He could not see anything but blackness and could barely breathe for the sack that was over his head, taped to his neck. Voices he could hear of some Middle Eastern sort. He could make nothing out. He decided to just lie there and make it as though he was still drugged and incapacitated. His wrists and ankles were bound by what felt like duct tape, and he had no shoes on. He heard the voices drawing near. This time, there was a hint of Mandarin that he could understand.

"Zhe ge ren ni yao xiaoxin. Ta shi you lianluo." Be careful with this guy; he has connections. He smiled in spite of himself; he was glad to finally be able to understand something. He was transported into one of the buildings by two strong men who carried him by his arms and legs. They dropped him a few times, and he had to strain so as not to grunt or give away his consciousness.

He was placed on some sort of a mattress or cushion on the floor, and the door closed behind the exiting transporters. Struggle as he might, there was no way he could get his wrists free. He had managed to untape part of the sack from around his neck, but for the wrists, he would have to wait. He listened. He waited. Thirty minutes. Two hours. How long, he could only guess. He began to hear quite a lot as he quieted his thoughts and focused his mind. He could hear the sounds of the cars outside and the wind blowing past the window. It was pretty warm, and he began to sweat. A thought crept into the corner of his mind. The hallway, the experience he had at home prior to the attack... Was there any way he could do that again?

Just as the thought appeared in his mind, the door was opened. He heard footsteps coming toward him. His bonds were removed, and his sack taken off. He kept his eyes shut to maintain the illusion of sleep but was rudely awakened by a boot to the stomach. He struggled for nearly a minute to regain his breath, all the while rolling and thrashing about, pounding on his chest. When he finally did find his breath, he looked around the room. There was one man standing above him with a gun in his hand.

In rather clean English, the man said, "So, tell me of your connections to the traitor..."

"What?" he thought. "Who is the traitor he was talking about?"

He looked up and said, "Where are we?" Another kick to the stomach, this time only about twenty seconds of pain. Again, the English: "You know of whom I speak, Dr. Campbell? The one who betrayed us, the one you know."

"I'm sorry, I have no idea what you are talking about, who you are, and what you are doing. Who are you?" He was trying hard not to tear up from the pain in his stomach. He wanted to avoid any sign of weakness that might lead the brutal captor to some sort of torture. His thoughts were suddenly awash with a series of images that flipped through his mind's eye like a picture album: images of mangled and tortured men held captive for information.

Again, a kick, but this time, the dentist was ready for it. He grabbed the man's foot with his still-bound hands and, carrying it in one continuous arcing motion from the kicker's intended path, lifted it high above his head as he began to stand up. This threw the attacker off balance, and he went toppling over in a shriek of agony when a frightening pop dislocated his femur from the hip. He groaned a few times and then began to reach for his gun.

John instinctively kicked the man as hard as he could in the head over and over. Shocked at the rage he had unleashed on this man, he waited for him to wake back up. As he stood over him, John began working on his wrists. He chewed and stripped the duct tape from his wrists until he could finally break the bonds. He rubbed his wrists for a while as he regained his composure.

Checking the unconscious man's pulse, he decided he needed to restrain the monster and took the roll of duct tape that had been on the desk outside the room. He wrapped him so tightly that he couldn't move much at all, he placed his hands and feet at opposite ends of the room and tied his feet up to the bars across the window. He placed one strip of tape across the man's mouth and picked up his gun. He fished around in his pockets and found a wallet, a cell phone, a butterfly knife, and an extra magazine of bullets. He took them all and then looked around the room. Where was his bag?

Opening the door, he was cautious to survey the room outside for any sign of movement. None. He stepped outside and nearly tripped over his bag. Opening it, he found all that was there when he left home. His tools, phone, snacks. He turned to the desk that was outside the room he had been in to find a photograph of himself standing next to a Taiwanese woman. He instantly recognized the photograph as one taken when he was a missionary at the Museum of Art and the woman as a previous mayor of Taichung City. It was a purely coincidental picture. Two foreign missionaries were at the city museum and found that the mayor of the city was there, so a picture was taken. It is one of those pictures that grandchildren ask about, and grandparents sometimes struggle to recall the details around. Is this who he was talking about? The traitor? What had he stumbled into...

Looking through the rooms in the apartment, he found that there were three rooms aside from the main living room and kitchen. One room where he had been held was very small, approximately 10 feet by 10 feet. The other two rooms were approximately the same size; one had two sets of bunk beds inside, and the other contained only a long table and several chairs around it. He walked through each of the rooms, searching for any information that might be helpful to him. All he could find were a large pile of stinking dirty clothes, numerous cigarette butts, several changes of clothing piled across the beds, and a nice-looking worn briefcase atop the table in the "office" room.

He walked toward the front of the apartment, where he came across several pairs of sandals arranged neatly facing into the apartment. The front door was a sliding glass one, much like the back door of an American home, with a double glass door. There was a small space, approximately 4 feet by 15 feet, that had nothing but windows and screens, with a security door on the right. Looking out of the window, he stared for a few moments, trying to imagine where he was when suddenly it came to him: he was in Taiwan! The beautiful mountains off in the distance, with the mists hanging over the city, and the sounds, the humidity. How had he ended up here? Kidnapped and in Taiwan? His mind began racing, searching for a solution, any reason, anything logical for his being there.

He remembered the van and remembered the car drive before that; he remembered back to the conversations with the detective and the man in the white sedan following him. In his mind's eye, he saw the porcelain slab smashing into the face of the man in his house.

Unbelievable. He stood in utter amazement, gazing out across the cityscape of Dali City, Taichung County, Taiwan.

Stunned for just a moment, he began to feel a presence. Sensing someone approaching the front door, he frantically searched for a hiding place or means of escape. Finally, he positioned himself behind the front door. A key was inserted into the lock and clicked, then turned, releasing the latch of the outer door. The door swung open, and a very tall man started to step through.

Instinctively, John braced himself against the wall and pushed with all his might against the door. The man, caught totally off guard, was smashed against the doorframe and fell clumsily and unconscious to the entryway floor.

"What have I done?" he thought to himself as he secured another man with tape and dragged his unconscious body into a different room. He had to get out of there. He took the new gun and the new cell phone, stuffed them in his bag, and exited the front door, borrowing a set of sandals on his way out.

Chapter 9
Appropriate Measures?

Jamison sat staring at his laptop, still surprised by the information he had discovered. He had been advised to stay away from classified materials unless they pertained directly to his target. This newfound information seemed to link his dentist friend to the terrorist ring. Somewhere, there was a connection to the dentist, but he couldn't find it.

He had the cell phone, the PDA, and more information than he had the previous night, but still not enough to piece everything together. Why had the terrorists taken this guy hostage? Why not just kill him? Why bring him to Taiwan? What was it about this man that threatened them? Usually, if someone knew something about the terrorist cell and the cell found out, they would ruthlessly kill the informant and the source. The vindictive words, "My cause is worth your life," popped into Jamison's mind.

Why, then, had they kept this American alive? The question bothered him like a fiberglass sliver under the skin—a constant and painful nuisance.

Jamison had been sent out in the field to capture a corrupt businessman and a terrorist striking a deadly deal. The agency would then move in with the new information to put both behind bars indefinitely, all the while extracting useful information from the terrorist and his pawn.

What had actually happened was very perplexing, indeed. At the moment when the handoff was supposed to take place, a catastrophic collapse of the adjacent building occurred. The building owner, who was not supposed to be involved, showed up in a frightful rage and was assassinated by his business partner while the third man, the one in the hospital, hopefully still alive, watched. Wen Zhang had somehow directed his buddies in the terrorist group to a dentist in the USA, and they had kidnapped him, bringing him to Taiwan.

How could the situation have gone sideways any faster? His cell phone buzzed in his pocket, and he flipped it open. Wei?

His contact relayed the information he had requested— information concerning the National Security Council and the Department of Homeland Security. There was credible information to suggest that a terrorist group funded by various organizations based in the Middle East, with ties to al-Qaeda, had built a small nuclear device and was attempting to import it for use on American soil. This device was reportedly small enough to fit into a backpack or small bag, making it easily disguised and hidden in any standard vehicle or transport container. The information also suggested that it would be deployed at a gathering of mass proportions to cause the most human damage possible.

Jamison shared the information with his handler about the dentist and the botched handoff, expressing his belief in a strong connection to the nuclear investigation. The handler responded coldly and tersely: "Leave it alone, Jamison. You're out of your league. You're a gatherer of information, not a black ops agent. We have intel from this morning placing the device entering the country from Yemen, not the Orient. We've taken appropriate measures."

With that, the conversation ended.

"Appropriate measures?" Jamison thought angrily. "The money was paid out to my target, my man," he reasoned. "Why would the money go to Wen Zhang, who was in Taiwan, while the services come from Yemen? Sure, Wen Zhang had spent a few years there while Robert Liu was initiating his shipping supply company, but if I were him, I would want the package that I was responsible for delivering in my own hands the whole time. Until the moment it was delivered to the doorstep."

Angry at his contact, he redialed the number. "Jamison, we're finished with this conversation. Leave it alone, or you'll never see any real action again. I have it in my mind to bring you in for a desk job, the way you've botched your first op. Just finish your recon and come home."

Again, he hung up.

Furious, Jamison began to search through pages and pages of information about Wen Zhang's time in Yemen. Finding nothing notable, he painstakingly compared people who met in Yemen to present-day business associates who were in Taiwan. Jamison had taken quite a few photos of the men Wen Zhang spent time around and accessed the photos on his computer. After several hours of clicking photos, searching for names, and clicking more photos, he came upon one match: Mohammad Al-Akezemi. This man, fabulously wealthy, had met Wen Zhang years ago in Yemen. He was a billionaire oil prince with a luxury mansion outside of Gaoxiong, about 3 hours away by train.

That was the match; there was the connection. It had to be! These two were the match heads, the enactors, the enablers of the cell he had become entrenched in.

He wanted to try something, a very, very risky gamble. But first, he needed some preparation.

Chapter 10
A Flood of Memories

Dr. Campbell took the stairs down 11 flights to the basement level, where he searched for an exit. He found one exit that led out of the building near the guard room situated at the main entrance. There was no getting out without having to pass by this guard room. Surveillance equipment and a guard would be present, but whether the guard was attentive or sleeping would be a gamble. He probably worked for the bad guys anyway.

He decided on a different route when he stumbled upon a row of mopeds. He quickly searched for the moped covered in the most dust and carefully inspected its tires and brakes before taking out his lock picks. Flipping the ignition switch and engaging the brake, he prepared to jimmy the lock. He had been taught the skill while in Taiwan almost ten years ago by a master locksmith. The concept was simple: a series of tumblers preventing the central shaft from turning. Jiggle the tumblers until the right combination fell into place, and voila. He tried for about 5 minutes with no success.

Not so easy this time. He would have to individually activate each tumbler. He gently applied rotational pressure to the ignition shaft and carefully touched and pushed each tumbler until they clicked, in order from farthest to most superficial. As he pushed on the last tumbler, the ignition turned, and immediately the engine started.

He was so startled when the engine started that his hand slipped, and he sliced his right hand deeply, embedding the lock pick into the fleshy part of his thumb. He shrieked and withdrew the pick. He was bleeding, and the pain was intense. He took the roll of duct tape out of his bag, trying not to bleed on everything, and tightly taped his hand to stop the bleeding. Then he hopped on the moped, trying not to wince every time he pulled the throttle.

The exit ramp of the garage had a sensor that triggered the security door, allowing the vehicles inside to exit without showing any ID or keying in the security passcode.

John blasted out of the garage without a second glance. He headed deep into the city, far away from the apartment complex. He drove for about 30 minutes and then needed to stop and refuel. He pulled into a filling station and filled the tank using money from a wallet he had taken from one of his kidnappers. Heading northward, he searched for anything that looked familiar. Nothing. He drove a bit further and then stopped.

He had stopped on a sort of bridge that curved as it passed over a set of train tracks, allowing him to see off into the distance. He stared for the longest time at the mountains to the east, reminiscing about a time when he had been there, in the mountains, with a completely different frame of mind.

He contemplated the time he had spent as a missionary, committed but largely unprepared for the two-year experience that would usher him into maturity and manhood. He remembered the first evening he slept in Taiwan, lying on the top bunk, wide awake at 3 a.m., looking out the window. He couldn't recall if it was the jet lag or the sheer excitement of the new culture that kept him awake. He thought back to the next several days of training and the experiences that unfolded, leading to a difficult and disconcerting realization. While at the Missionary Training Center in Provo, he had been completely excited to go out and do what missionaries do: speak with anyone who would give him the time of day. Yet, upon arriving in Taiwan and actually approaching people—complete strangers, entirely foreign to him—he realized that this was not the walk in the park he had envisioned earlier.

Missionary work proved to be very difficult, especially for an introvert. Standing on the bridge, he recalled the constant, ubiquitous struggle he had faced during his two years as a missionary in this very city. He loved the work, cherished the gospel of Jesus Christ, and enjoyed learning the language, but he struggled immensely with stepping outside of himself and speaking with everyone he met.

Staring off into the distance, he felt a flood of warmth as he recalled the feelings of being released as a missionary. He had sacrificed for all those many months, done the best he could each day, and had a great sense of gratitude for the experiences he had, the growth and maturation he had seen, and the lives that had been touched, most of all his own.

He started the moped again and sped off. He had carefully chosen an older model of moped because the key was not for the ignition switch. The key only needed to be unlocked once, and then the switch pressed to start the little motor over and over.

He stopped to ask for directions to the city center of Taichung and to find out where he was.

The woman was ancient. She had been walking down the side of the street, just next to the open sewer, sort of hobbling with her right hand on her hip. She was dressed in a flowered blouse, sort of bluish, with white lilies and dark pants. Her hair was short, and her dentition was nearly completely missing, yet she smiled as John politely asked:

"Qing wen, xiaojie, qing wen!" (Miss, miss, one question, please). Her smile turned into a sort of scowl as she heard the broken yet passable Mandarin spoken by a foreigner. Her response was in Taiwanese, a similar, yet completely different version of spoken Mandarin. She mumbled the directions and waved a finger off to the north, or what John assumed to be the north, then continued walking along her pathway without a second thought for the tall white man with short dark hair who seemed unshaven and in desperate need of a shower.

He had never been very fluent in the Taiwanese language. He never really needed to learn it, as most of the people in Taiwan spoke Mandarin Chinese, the national language of China.

However, there was a rather large population of the elderly who only spoke Taiwanese, although they, for the most part, could understand pretty much everything in Chinese as well.

John headed northward on the next main street he could find and pledged to drive until he found his friends, the Pings.

As he drove, he passed many shops along the road. The larger roads contained mainly nicer, more franchise-type shops and stores, filled with various sundries from Q-tips to flip-flops, while the smaller roads consisted of a multitude of small, unique, family-owned shops. Most of the thoroughfares, whether wide or narrow, were lined with these shops and stores, as well as motorcycle repair shops, cafés, grocers, and booksellers. These little shops were the epitome of community and neighborhood identity. John thought back again to the two years he lived there, to the hours he spent on foot and bicycle walking and riding past these wonderful places. Oftentimes, they would spend much of their days in and out of the unique shops, conversing with the owners and employees and looking. Just looking at the merchandise.

Many of these shops were set up on the ground floor of the

building, with the family who owned and operated the shop living on the second and third levels. Often, the sundries were covered with dust, and the expiration dates were crossed out with a marker, perhaps as an attempt to conceal overstocked family-owned inventory. These were wonderful little places where you could actually barter with the owner over an apple, a guava, or a mango. Much negotiation and relationship-building took place. It was easy to develop a close bond with the man who owned the grocery store in his front room across the street or the woman who pushed her fruit cart around every morning at 6:30, offering fresh mangos and pineapples. These people were the lifeblood of the community, representing the identity of those who lived there. Yet, much of Taiwan was transitioning to a more "mainstream" type of commerce system, where huge corporations moved in and squeezed every last penny out of the family-owned businesses.

Such a travesty, he thought as the palm trees whizzed past. He had come out of the city and was on a more open road heading toward another sprawling center of commerce and industrialism. His hand began to throb again; he needed some medical attention before something got infected, and he had some serious issues to deal with.

He carefully looked left and right as he buzzed down the street. He noticed a tall building on the right and sensed some familiarity with the surroundings. When he reached the building's rear side, he stopped and pulled off to the sidewalk, leaning his moped on the kickstand.

He looked around him and began to remember some memory, some distant relic of recognition. Suddenly, he recognized a hospital where he had been a patient almost 15 years ago. He walked around to the front of the hospital and stood wide-eyed for a moment. As he stood, both feet planted on the pavement, he began to have another flashback of the days he spent in Taiwan. This flashback was more intense and more personal, though.

The sight of the hospital, combined with the familiarity of the smells and people, triggered a cascade of unimaginable events. It was as if he had been placed inside a movie of himself and his surroundings as a missionary. He could see himself, feel what it felt like, observe how others reacted to him, and experience the feelings that they were feeling. Memory after memory and image after image slid past his eyes. He began to tremble as the remembrance of those days was so strong. Instantly, a wave of emotion flooded through his body. His entire being was suddenly wrapped in the most wonderful sense of accomplishment and love. The string of memories was cathartic and refreshing as he recalled the time he had spent in self-denying service.

After recovering from his experience, he continued into the hospital and toward the emergency department he had once visited as a young man with a basketball-related nose injury. It was strangely empty as he passed through the doors. One nurse looked up from her desk when he walked by, but she dismissed him summarily as if he was not out of place at all. He cautiously found a supply closet and began to search for sutures, antiseptics, and antibiotics. The closet was more of a supply warehouse and seemed to stretch forever, so he easily located his needed supplies. Retiring to the bathroom, he prepared himself for the experience.

With his left hand, he carefully poured some Betadine antiseptic over the deep cut. The solution seared the nerve endings, and John winced in an effort to remain quiet. The burning was awful. He had been unlucky enough to come upon an empty box marked "lidocaine," so much for anesthesia. As the burning continued, he began to carefully stitch the deep tissue layer back together. Stopping to blot away the blood, he could see that the deeper muscle of the hand had been torn, and to maximize healing, he needed to repair the deeper laceration before approximating the superficial skin layer. It took him 23 stitches in total to repair the laceration, each stitch inflicting slightly less pain as he slowly grew accustomed to the needle piercing the flesh. The most difficult part was tying the knots at the end. Nylon was notorious for unraveling, so several extra throws of the surgeon's knot were necessary. Doing this one-handed, with his teeth as an assistant, and being left-handed made it very difficult.

He completed the sutures and again splashed Betadine over the barely acceptably repaired gash. He tucked the Betadine and an extra package of sterile gauze into his backpack and happened to catch sight of the gun from the corner of his eye. A cold shiver ran down his spine.

Deciding to take a different way out, just to avoid any possible second thoughts from the nurse he had passed earlier, he headed across the large waiting room toward a set of double doors.

Chapter 11
Chou Do Fu

As he passed through the double doors, he was met with the backs of a huge crowd of reporters and onlookers, apparently concerned with one of the patients staying in an adjacent sick bed. He managed to stroll through the crowd undetected until he had almost reached the far wall. One of the reporters was making some sort of live broadcast and mentioned the name "Zhang Yi-Cheng" as the patient. Instantly, Dr. Campbell stopped dead in his tracks.

"What?" he said out loud. "Could that possibly be Yi Cheng?" A couple of members of the crowd turned to look at him, and he dismissed them and pressed through the large gathering once again.

The one who sent him the emails and the pictures? He instantly turned his focus to the story narrated by one of the news reporters who was on live camera. The short, lithe Taiwanese man spoke of a building collapse, a suicide, and a subsequent attempted poisoning right here at the hospital. Dumbfounded, John stood and stared. Suicide? Poisoning? Who would want to poison someone that was… The spinning cogs in his mind slowly came to a screeching halt… Could it be possible that Yi

Cheng is being trailed by the same monsters that are on my tail? How could that be?

John instinctively knew that if he stayed there, he was in danger. Perhaps the men who had orchestrated his kidnapping were now aware of his escape and flight. Possibly, there were lookouts placed here at the hospital and elsewhere. He had to get out, and get out fast.

Searching for an exit, he turned in a full circle to take in his surroundings. He had been heading for an exit near the emergency department but felt that way would most likely be watched. Suddenly, a memory flashed through his mind of a corridor in this very hospital that led to the psych ward where he had offered his services years before. Gaining his bearings, he located the corridor and began to swiftly move toward the exit. As he did, he caught the glance of another man who was near the exit he had previously desired to reach. Instantly, the man began to move toward him and brought some sort of radio to his mouth.

John bolted at that second for the corridor, knowing that there would be several exits once he reached the hallway. He passed through the opening and turned the corner at breakneck speed, only to run headlong into a nurse with a cart of supplies. Various medical supplies were thrown into the air as the surprised nurse screamed and hopped out of the way of the large American. He regained his composure and again bolted down the hallway.

This hallway made several turns as it snaked its way from the main medical plaza to the psych ward of the hospital, harboring many sets of attached chairs for those who would wait for various appointments and checkups. He found a large pillar about midway down the corridor and pulled himself behind it into the shadows. He tried to quiet himself behind the large concrete column but was out of breath from the sudden jolt of adrenaline and subsequent burst of speed. He was not as in shape as he had been at one point in his life and regretted it more now than ever.

Reaching inside his backpack that he had loaded prior to being kidnapped and shanghaied to Taiwan, he was amazed to find the bag had not been violated since he began this adventure, and he hoped his supplies were still intact. His hand found the handgun he had taken from one of the guards, and he gripped it tightly. Bringing it to bear, he silently removed the magazine and verified the status of the rounds within. The palm of his hand began to throb from his previous injury and self-inflicted repair. He reinserted the clip, pulled back the slide, and released it, bringing a live round into the chamber. He then checked to see that the safety was off and waited as silently as possible. He had never been in this type of situation before, with someone trying to kill him and a handgun loaded in his hand. It was pretty frightening and brought to the surface many feelings of inadequacy, fear, and retrospective disdain for some of his previous actions. He had the distinct feeling that he may not ever see his wife and children again. He closed his eyes in an attempt to ward off the fears, but instead, he began to feel. He didn't understand why, but he again began to feel what was happening around him.

The hallway was quiet, with the air carrying a slight tinge of dust and oil. He could feel the press of humidity and the beating of his own heart within him. Peering around the corner of the column, he sensed that the man was not too far away.

He could see that the man was across the corridor, crouched behind a set of chairs, mostly concealed. He could see the gun, the clothes, the hair, and the expression on the man's hateful face. With his right hand, he had the grip of the gun held firmly, perhaps too firmly.

As John was considering his next move, he heard a sudden ripping sound followed by a loud thud as his bag fell to the ground. He was so startled that he didn't know what to do and was caught totally off guard. He had been holding his backpack by the zipper, with his middle finger anchored in a small hole in the fabric. This hole had been acquired during an organic chemistry lab session when he had spilled red-hot sand from a test tube heater on his bag. The sand melted right through the fabric and also scorched some of his expensive chemistry books. He was forever finding sand particles in his homework and sack lunches. The fabric had begun to strain under the weight of the load and had all at once given way to a massive tear parallel to the zipper, running down to the base of the bag. The tear had shifted the weight, and the bag had instantly slipped from its perch, landing loudly on the floor in front of the surprised dentist.

His concentration was totally gone, and he could hear the other man approaching him. In his startled state, he accidentally squeezed the trigger and released a high-velocity round of copper and lead down the corridor in front of him. Instantly, the assailant returned fire, or rather joined the firing, and began squeezing rounds off down the hallway in the same direction as the round John had fired. Surprised, John just sat there.

The pursuer realized that John was somewhere in the shadows and took to the shadows. Silence. John decided that he would much rather be away from the situation than have to kill this man, so he began to think of ways to simply get out. Fortunately for him, a security guard began to approach the two secreted men, bringing all the attention to himself. The frightened nurse had summoned a rent-a-cop, and now the end of the hallway was also filled with the reporters who had been there for another reason.

The man pursuing John slipped out and down the hallway away from the commotion. John decided to take an exit immediately opposite the location the pursuer had taken and also disappeared. He headed out into the night. There was plenty of light in the street as he made his way around to the front of the hospital, where he had parked his moped. He had pulled a hat out of his backpack and tried to change his appearance slightly to foil his follower.

Finding the moped, he gently and quickly jimmied it again and buzzed away down the narrow city streets toward the home of his friends, the Ping family. He knew they would be able to help and provide him with some sort of shelter, at least for the time being, while he figured out what was happening to him.

Jamison sat, staring at the cell phone he had been tinkering with for the last few minutes. His idea was to send a simple text message to the phone, stating the need to talk with the prisoner for a few moments. He had prepared the message several times and then deleted it, not quite mentally ready for what might happen. Previously, he had arranged several cameras in a small restaurant for just a moment like this. If he could somehow pressure the kidnappers into bringing the hostage to the restaurant, he could glean some valuable information.

"Meet with the prisoner at Wu Quan Road, #498-12. In the restaurant, upper-level private dining room #5. 7 pm. Al-Akezemi."

He waited.

John continued buzzing through the city, passing by the large discothèques and various shopping centers that occupied this higher-end part of town. One of the cell phones in his bag buzzed and chimed, but it wasn't loud enough to attract his attention over the hum of the engine. He was in familiar territory now, driving down Zhong San Lu past the towering commerce buildings and the numerous shops that inhabited this neck of the woods. He came to a large intersection, which housed a tall statue of a man pushing what appeared to be a large, many-toothed wheel up an incline. He remembered the many times he had passed through this intersection during previous missionary efforts.

He passed a boys' prep school on the right side of the street, backed up against a number of housing complexes. There was a small alleyway just to the north of the school through which he had biked many times before. He had another flashback of passing the school, making the hard-right turn, and weaving in and out of the pedestrians as they traversed the city. There were usually several large flat baskets set out on top of the cars in the alley, filled with freshly cut Doufu (Tofu) and placed in the sun to dry and cure. Another motorist cut very close to him and brought his attention back to the road ahead.

He passed the large stadium that housed a full-size track and had a grassy area in the center where he used to play soccer and football on his days off. There were so many memories of this place, so many amazing memories that he had not been aware of until his return. He made another right turn and passed over several large sets of train tracks. He stopped to gain his bearings. It had been many, many years since he had been to this apartment complex, and he had difficulty remembering which of the host of buildings it was that the Pings lived in. He puttered around for a few minutes until he saw something that was familiar. Parking his bike, he entered the apartment complex and began to walk toward the elevators.

There had been an earthquake a few years back, and he remembered seeing pictures in the news of many tall-rise buildings that had been affected by the tremors. Some thousands of people had died, and many buildings had been declared uninhabitable.

He ascended to the 12th floor after trying the 10th and 11th floors with no success. There it was, the Pings' home. There were four doors to various apartments on this level, each with a host of flip-flops and shoes surrounding the door. He approached the door and rapped on the cool steel three times. No answer. He waited, then knocked again three times. Still, no answer. He wondered if they were still at work at this late hour of the evening. He sat down and began to dig through his bag for something edible. As he sat, he heard a chime from one of the cell phones that he had confiscated.

Opening the message, he sat in shock as he read the message:

"Meet with the prisoner at Wu Quan Road, #498-12. In the restaurant, upper-level private dining room #5. 7 pm. Al-Akezemi."

Who was Al-Akezemi? Was he the prisoner? He thought for a moment that if he could just clear up the matter, they might leave him alone. He highlighted the "sent from" number and pressed the green call key.

Chapter 12
Who Are You?

Suddenly, the phone rang. It was not some sort of message but an incoming call. What had he done? If he didn't answer the phone and convincingly play the role of a terrorist, then his neck was on the line. He answered in the best Arabic-accented Chinese he could muster: "Wei?"

The caller spoke in Chinese: "Who are you?" Silence followed.

Jamison's mind raced. How was he going to get out of this one? He spoke as coolly as possible in Mandarin: "I am in charge of this operation, and I demand to see the infidel who has compromised my plan. Are you Al-Akezemi? Are you the monster who ordered this hell unleashed on some poor innocent bystander you call an infidel?"

"What?" Jamison recoiled at the angry reply. It made no sense unless...

"John?" he spoke in English. "Are you Dr. John Campbell?" Silence followed.

"How did you... who are you?" he said in English.

Jamison was taken aback by the prospect that an untrained dentist had been able to elude his captors. He began explaining from the beginning of the story, leaving out anything classified and outlining most of the big picture. Jamison was a CIA field agent placed in Taiwan to monitor and document an exchange. The exchange involved a payment for a mode of transport. There was a terrorist faction positioned in Taiwan, prepared to make some sort of acquisition of a nuclear device. They had destroyed a building and were close to accomplishing their plan of purchasing transportation for their nuclear device into the US, subsequently unleashing destruction and needless killing on an unimaginable scale. He explained that John had been brought into the mess through the emails Yi Cheng had sent him, and somehow, the terrorists had tracked him down, thinking he was aware of and involved in a plot to thwart their plan.

He listened as John recounted his harrowing experience with the assassin in his home, the attack, his flight from his family, and how he had finally been transported to Taiwan and subsequently managed to escape several attackers, putting him where he was now.

Jamison sat in sheer amazement, stunned by the tale of the escape from the attackers' bonds. He was dumbfounded and had no idea what to do other than to offer his assistance to the unfortunate dentist who happened to receive the wrong email at the wrong time.

After a moment of thought, he decided that they needed to meet. Arrangements were made to meet the following morning.

———

John had just hung up the phone and turned it off when he heard the elevator motor begin to hum and whirr. He stepped up to the landing in the stairwell, where he could be hidden but still ascertain the identity of those ascending in the elevator, should they decide to get off on this level.

The elevator dinged, and the doors slid open. He couldn't tell who they were but immediately sensed a presence, a friendly and familiar presence. They chatted quietly about some event's occurrence, and he could barely make out their voices. Then he knew it. He knew who it was. With a wide smile on his face, he went bounding down the stairs.

The residents of the building immediately went ghost-white as they saw the tall white man come down the stairs. Then, the father's jaw dropped. It took him a while to catch his breath before he let out: "Ke Zhang Lao! Hao Jiu Bu Jian!" (Elder Campbell, long time no see!) 'Elder' was the title given to missionaries and also the name this family knew John by.

What followed was a truly joyous reunion. John had been away for so very long, and with the new dental practice needing much babysitting and attention, he had been entirely unable to slip away and visit his second homeland, Taiwan. The Ping family was more than overjoyed to see him; they were totally surprised but happy and grateful nonetheless. Their children were grown now; one daughter was 18, the other almost 7. They spoke for the longest time, deep into the early hours of the morning, about times long past, about experiences each had enjoyed in the time they had been apart. The Ping family adopted John as a virtual son, seeing that they only had daughters and that they held a very special place for him in their hearts. John had done the same, considering them a part of his family. Each was so grateful to see the other. Many tears were shed at this meeting of friends and separated family members. Tears of joy.

John explained the reasons for his being there and the unbelievable story of his escape and contact with the CIA. By this time, it was nearly 2 am, and everyone was completely exhausted from the evening's surprises. John asked for the couch for the night and was offered the couch for the rest of his life, should he desire it.

As he lay on the semi-comfortable couch, his mind was full. Full of a thousand images of the people there, the families he knew and missed, the experiences he had enjoyed, and the hardships he had faced being thrust into a new culture and environment. He thought of the challenges he faced as a young missionary: learning the five-toned Mandarin Chinese with its many inflections and intonations, learning the cultures of the people and their traditions, coming face to face with himself and his abilities, and learning that he could push himself beyond his own limits when he had the incentive and was aware of the possible outcomes of his actions. He remembered and reconfirmed the assistance, even the constant help and support of his Father in Heaven, and was grateful for the learning and growing experience he had endured.

He thought back to one of his early experiences in Taiwan: an evening on a train, his first ever train ride in all of his life. He could see the images, smell the smells, and feel the wind on his face as though he were in the midst of the experience right now. He could see the moon over the countryside, highlighting just enough of the terrain to make out a house here, a rice paddy there, a gathering of homes, and a desolate road. He could see the stands of bamboo bending in the wind and hear the train cars jostling with one another. He remembered the thoughts that flew through his mind that night as he headed south from Taichung to the little township of Chaozhou in Pingtung Xian. He recalled thinking that he was now thousands of miles away from his family and knew little to nothing about Chinese and Taiwanese people, culture, and language. Yet he was so excited, armed with a deep commitment to his faith and his desire to serve.

He remembered sitting on the bike rack of a more experienced missionary who carried him to his new home.

He awoke to the smell of cooking eggs and hot doujiang (soy milk). It was nearly 7 am, and he had to meet with Jamison at 9:30. He hurriedly ran into the bathroom and did his best to wash up and prepare himself for another day of running and espionage.

Chapter 13
An Offer He Simply Could Not Refuse

Wen Zhang sat at his desk, astounded and surprised at the report he had just received from the terrorist contact. Aside from the break-in at his apartment, someone had broken into the safe house and rescued the hostage. He pondered for a few moments about the CIA presence he had noticed, with all the cameras and bugging devices placed around his apartment and at the office. Perhaps it was the American CIA.

He had thought for a long time that there would be some undercover and clandestine awareness of his participation with the terrorist group. He was really only in it for the money. He had worked long and hard and really never made any money. It was his turn to be rich, and he wanted to be filthy rich.

What would happen if perhaps his little world of espionage and terrorism came crashing down around him? He had never really contemplated too much. At times, he had imagined being caught and incarcerated, but most of the time, he just blocked out the possible consequences of his actions. How had he come this far, he thought…At one time, I was a loving family man with kids and a loving wife.

He began to remember the sweeter times in his life when he had something to come home to, something to enjoy and cherish. It had all begun to deteriorate ever so slowly when he first came across a magazine while traveling. It had been left on a chair in an airport somewhere, and he had sat obliviously next to it for the longest time. He set his newspaper down on the chair next to him, and when he stood up to leave, he must have picked it up as well. At first, it was shocking, but at the same time, very exciting. He had taken the magazine to his hotel, where he had thrown it in the trash, but later given in to the temptation and dug it out of the garbage to peruse its filthy and disgusting pages.

Slowly and steadily, he began to feel the effects of an initially mild addiction to the stuff, but as he consciously continued to casually partake, it grabbed hold of him in such a way he could not easily break free. Many times, he had spoken with others about self-control and the need for discipline, and many times, he had committed and made promises to himself, just himself, that he would change.

He came back to reality for just a moment as he felt a slight twinge of heat and pain in his chest. He had been enduring some heart problems, mostly a severe blockage of his Left Anterior Descending branch of the coronary artery that would really cause him pain from time to time, especially when he was stressed or overexerted.

He again remembered back to those weeks and months when he fought with his animal nature and committed, recommitted, and again recommitted himself to virtue. His repeated failure to follow through and his constant lusts brought him to seek out that which he would have disdained and spurned just a few years earlier in his life. He began to look for those places of entertainment that catered to men whose lusts had manipulated, monopolized, and mangled their lives. He would make excuses and tell lies that he repeatedly told his wife, and he thought that she probably believed him in the beginning. He would schedule a business meeting or some sort of business trip, and then he would reschedule the meetings or skip them so that he could entertain his covetous lusts and pathetic desires.

He could tell that he was hurting his wife and his children, but still, he gave in. Eventually, she divorced him, took the kids, and left. He kept in touch just to make sure the kids knew that he loved them, but at one point, he was so totally consumed with himself that he neglected and forgot them completely. He missed their birthdays, games, and performances and totally forgot about them. For years, he lived only for himself and his addictions. Every penny that wasn't sent for alimony or child support went to his addictions and his self-indulgence.

One morning, he found himself strung out and hung over on the floor of a strip club. It was at that point that something inside of him broke, and he became totally numb. It was also on that morning that he no longer had any desire to pursue his lusts but only to see his children, whom he had totally neglected for several years. Although he had lost the desire, he still had to confront the physical addictions. These addictions were so severe and so entwined within him that he required rehab and therapy to break them.

He thought his addictions to drugs and alcohol would be much different to overcome compared to his addiction to sex. In reality, it was the sex addiction that proved the most formidable. Every day, every moment, and every situation would trigger a thought, an image, a reaction that he initially could not control. Even after the therapy and the hypnotism, he would still fight ferociously to overcome the desires that ravaged and ruined his self-esteem and his life. It was at that point that he realized he actually had passions again—passions that were good and purposeful.

After a complete turnaround in his life and much intensive counseling, he was able to break free from the flaxen cords of pornography, drugs, and alcohol. It was not a one-time, total success; it was more of a low-level, constant, yet life-threatening battle that raged every single day. Every stimulus, whether visual, audio, or otherwise, would initially evoke a response. He would focus and focus, chant and pray, and slowly, the layers of adhesive would wear away.

Eventually, he reached the point where his life was clean. He was back to the point where he would not feel disgusting if he were to sit in the same room as his children and his ex-wife. The only way he made it was to carry a small photo of the children with him everywhere. Each time the temptation would surface, the thoughts return, and the desires come, he would pull the picture out of his pocket and chant to himself, "I can do it for my children, I can do it for my children, I can do it for my children…" and on and on. There were often times in his meetings when he would be caught totally off guard and unprepared while staring at the picture.

He had tried to reestablish contact with his family, but his ex-wife had kept him at a distance, and for good reason. He had destroyed their marriage and, with it, the stability that their children needed to provide them with a solid foundation of love and respect that they so desperately needed to navigate their way through life. It was too late; besides, the damage was irreparable. His daughters were disgusted by the thought of how their father had come home in the evenings—drunk, stinking, and high. Often, he would come home with the smell of some other woman about him.

It was too late. The relationships he had created were impetuously and completely destroyed. Instead of spending each of the extra few moments he had between work and sleep with his children, fostering love or instilling virtue, or just spending a few minutes of together time, he would opt out of his responsibilities and turn to the internet, the bottle, or the syringe. He had disrespected everything he held important—the fidelity of his wife, the trust of his daughters, and the respect of his son—and they wanted nothing to do with him now.

He looked up from his desk to the photo hanging over the mantle. The smiling family he once knew. Regret so deep and cutting took hold of his heart that he hung his head a moment in silence and utter remorse. Had he not totally blocked off any and all human expression from his life, perhaps he would have cried.

After the final rejection from his family, he fell into a deep depression and began to abuse only the office. He spent every waking moment at the office, a nice cushy administrative position for a local property management company. It was then that the building had been purchased by Robert, and his life began to change. He met his second wife at a company retreat, and they had instantly fallen in love. Merely eight months later, he became aware of the affair with Robert and confronted her about it. She chuckled and said, "Well, what did you expect when you married me, that I would be perfect like you?"

It was only fitting that he be treated as such after obliterating his family with his destructive and maniacal lusts. So now, he had endured, if only to some small degree, that hell which he had inflicted upon his family. Oh, how he hated himself more every day.

His heart had grown so callous that he no longer cared about anything. His family had abandoned him, his newfound love and wife had an affair with his boss, and he was beginning to have heart problems. All that he wanted at this point in his painful life was a little comfort. He just didn't care about anything else.

Late last year, he traveled to Yemen to do business with Robert. It was there that a wealthy oil prince had made him an offer that he simply could not refuse: a huge amount of money for only one small transport container. Initially, he had thought that they would only want to smuggle in supplies or literature or perhaps drugs. He was pretty naïve, and he liked it that way.

Chapter 14
Wen Zhang Sat and Waited

John sat at the small corner restaurant for nearly an hour before he saw the man coming toward him. He waited patiently in the back corner of the small little fan dian (restaurant) and even ordered a bowl of chicken fried rice with some money he had borrowed from the Ping family. The rice was delicious and exactly as he remembered it. The cook dropped a whole clove of garlic into the boiling oil, then crushed it before adding the eggs, vegetables, and rice. He had tossed it completely out of the pan and up into the air before catching it again and mixing it with the ladle-type spoon he held in his right hand. It was truly an art. After cooking the rice, he piled it onto a plate and then gave the American a spoon to eat it with. John had asked for a pair of quai zi, and the cook gave him a peculiar look before fishing out a set of chopsticks from underneath the counter.

He sat and ate his rice, one chopstick full at a time, all the while contemplating what he needed to do and how he could resolve this mess that had come to him so rapidly. He slowly reenacted his experiences thus far in his mind, trying to make sense of the madness, trying to capture some sort of rational outcome that did not end in horrific bloodshed. How could he get out of this mess?

As he contemplated the scenario, he saw the man approaching. He was a rather tall man in his mid-30s with some wear and tear that showed on his hands and head as a bald spot. He was clean-shaven and had an air of professionalism about him. He came to the table with a steaming hot plate of rice in his hand and sat down across from John. They both ate in silence for a few moments. Each man sized up the other in a sort of mental weighing. John thought for a few moments that perhaps this supposed CIA agent was not who he said he was. He felt a slight chill run down his spine, and an idea began to take shape within his mind. Just then, Jamison spoke.

The conversation began in the most peculiar way, with Jamison speaking only in Mandarin. At first, John was startled, but then he seemed to be able to keep up rather well. They first discussed the reason for Jamison's being in Taiwan, in Taichung, and his understanding of the Cell that had kidnapped John. There were many words that John did not understand in Mandarin, as his previous experience and training with the language had been mostly religious in nature. After several apparently irritating queries, Jamison finally gave in and continued in English.

———

He asked the shocked American dentist about his captors. Had they said anything? Had they mentioned anything that may be revealing or otherwise suspicious? No. Had they taken him anywhere or made him do anything that would provide any hint of intel on what the plot was to make the nuclear device passable and portable? No.

Jamison then shared perhaps a little more than he should have as he told John of the information that indicated a probable attack on US soil. He went on about the group that had been identified in Kansas City and the agent that had infiltrated the group to uncover a long, convoluted plot to bring a disguised portable nuclear device into the US for use at a "mass gathering" of some sort. Again, continuing just a little too much, he spoke about the several playoff games remaining in the run-up to the Super Bowl, with one approaching tomorrow evening. The trick, he said, was that there was some difficulty in bringing the device through and past the border security. There had to be some deception, some great deception that would either create a massive diversion or appear so innocuous that no one would question the package.

Continuing, he mentioned the large transport container that had been procured by the Taiwanese cell for the supposed transport of the device into the US and dropped the name of Zhong You Mall, as he explained. It was mind-numbing to think of the nightmare that would soon come to pass unless the agency was able to intercept and disarm the device.

—————

"What?" John said, his mind reeling as he soaked in the words he had been listening to for nearly an hour now. He had always heard of the possibility of a nuclear attack but assumed that the materials, fuels, and expertise to create such a weapon were always under tight surveillance. He sat for what seemed like an eternity with Jamison staring at him impatiently. Gathering his wits about him, he tried to think back to the several hours he had spent conscious and waiting, tied up and gagged in the room, and the few minutes of conversation he had heard prior to his escape. Nothing came to mind, or at least nothing that he could remember anyway. He looked into the eyes of the agent and told him exactly that. He couldn't remember anything that might be useful in any way.

They discussed the situation at length and determined that John needed to lay low and Jamison needed to glean a little more information before they met next. Jamison said that he would call in another agent or two and try to get John on an escorted flight back to the US before anything else happened.

With that, they separated. It was nearly noon, and John was exhausted. He watched the agent speed off on the moped and thought of his transport back to the US tomorrow. He was to meet the agent at 7 am tomorrow to be escorted back to the US by yet another agent. "I'm not going until I visit one more friend," he thought. Speeding off toward the heart of Taichung City, he tried to visualize the roads he had traveled so many years ago to his friend Ernest's apartment.

Finally, the contact returned his call, and Wen Zhang hopped into his M3 and sped toward the mall. A large portion of the cleanup was done, and surprisingly enough, the other two buildings were open and functioning for business following an inspection approval from the Urban Development and Housing Authority. Pulling into his personal parking spot, he waved to one of the guards to come and open his door. He got out of the car and entered the building, heading toward the shipping docks where the container was to be loaded and supervised. Several men were waiting for him as he lumbered out of the elevator, his heart beginning to sting with angina from the stress. Three looked like normal Taiwanese workers, dressed in what appeared to be shop uniforms, but the other two seemed a bit more Middle Eastern than the average populace. They greeted him with business faces, revealing nothing but their own impatience and displeasure at his tardy arrival to the mall. Wen Zhang cleared the area of all personnel so that there would be no witnesses of anything except him.

After a few minutes of conversation with the foreigners about paperwork, times, and policies, one of the men stepped away and made a phone call. Within seconds, a full-sized semi-truck was backing into the shipping dock area toward the dock. It pulled up next to the truck that had been parked for some time.

After an hour of successfully transferring a huge number of

boxes from one truck to the other, the three workers headed off to their well-deserved smoke break.

One of the foreign men placed a brief phone call the moment the truck was loaded.

Wen Zhang had been sitting quietly in the shipping office, watching carefully through the thick safety glass as the workers loaded box after box after box into the large trailer truck. The boxes appeared to be retail items, including shirts, shoes, hats, watches, stuffed animals, and a host of other interesting and equally meaningless items. He had postulated that the item or items that were to be shipped would be cleverly disguised to avoid detection, but he hadn't thought that there would be so many boxes. It almost seemed like a legitimate shipment! Perhaps it was, he thought, perhaps it was. This truck was not headed to the seaport but to the airport. Its contents would be loaded on the next flight out, then off over the mighty Pacific Ocean to somewhere in what he presumed to be the USA. It was the shipping of whatever it was that would bring the corporation of Zhong You down. The expedited shipping bill was being paid by Robert's company. Wen Zhang was pretty sure that the package would be traced back to Robert, hence the arrangements and the placement of guilt on the dead man.

One of the men had climbed up into the now half-full truck and was inspecting the boxes closest to the back. He had pulled some papers from his briefcase and was marking off what appeared to be a shipping invoice. The other man stepped into the room with Wen Zhang and began speaking in less-than-fluent Mandarin. They were doing the final check of the loaded parcels and would be shipping out momentarily. He thanked Wen Zhang for his assistance and then reached deep into his inside jacket pocket. Wen Zhang immediately braced himself for what he assumed was the last thing he would ever see: the front end of a gun. To his surprise, rather than a handgun, the man withdrew a large envelope of what appeared to be cash, tossed it onto the desk in front of Wen Zhang, and then abruptly walked away.

Wen Zhang sat and waited for the sting in his heart to calm down. This time it didn't. He began to feel more and more pain, so he reached into his pocket, pulled out some Nitro pills, and popped a quick three-pill fix. Still feeling the pain, he fingered the envelope and withdrew the contents: a stack of $100 bills (USD) and an obviously intentionally placed photo of his family. His heart sank into the depths of his stomach at that moment. This was silence money, with a not-so-veiled threat attached. He knew that if he told anyone (not that he planned to), his mistake would be duly recompensed upon his family. His family. His heart could no longer bear it, and he had a heart attack. The pain was so intense, unlike any he had felt at any point in his life. His chest felt like it was going to explode. He lost his breath and never got it back as he sat grasping at his chest. The light in the room seemed to gradually grow dim, and he could hear a ringing in his ears that grew with each gasp for breath. He thought back to his children and their sweet faces. He thought back to the pain he had caused them. He settled on a memory of his eldest daughter in her first kindergarten music concert, the little white dress she had worn, and the smile on her face. With that, he relented to the pain and agony that had been continuously building to a horrible catharsis. He coughed once, a deep, guttural, agonal cough, and then lay back in his chair to die.

Chapter 15
Apathy and Soundproof Glass

It was nearly 2 pm by the time he located Shi Zong Road, deep in the heart of Taichung. He had forgotten most of the names of the roads and could only recall certain outstanding buildings and complexes adjacent to the various roads he was navigating. He could visualize the main thoroughfares and some of the smaller roads, but not to the extent that would guide him directly to his destination. He managed to stumble onto the road that housed the apartment his friend Ernest had lived in nearly ten years ago and wondered if he would even be there now. Ernest was on the fast track to a high-level management position with his schooling and his family background. He would likely be immediately inducted into the upper-level management of his family's restaurant business when he got out of school, assuming his choice to go to school didn't prevent that from happening. If he wasn't at the apartment, John knew there was a restaurant where he could gather some more information.

He ascended to the 8th floor of the elevator-less building and knocked on the door on the far left. An aging relic of a woman answered the door and muttered something in broken

Taiwanese. John asked politely if she happened to know where Earnest You was and then waited as she processed his broken Mandarin. She began to speak in Mandarin, choosing to ask him why a foreigner was in her country. She began to share her thoughts on the Japanese occupation of Taiwan decades ago and became quite long-winded.

John tried to patiently wait for an opportune moment to re-interject his query but was unsuccessful. He stared into the old woman's eyes and thought to himself that she probably never had anyone to talk to and so was taking advantage of this unique opportunity. Just as she was at the height of her explanation of Taiwanese and Japanese international relations, a surprisingly loud fart escaped from her backside. She was either totally unaware or completely mortified to the point that she didn't want to acknowledge what happened and so continued uninterrupted in her discourse. John, on the other hand, became entirely unable to prevent himself from breaking into a deep and cleansing laugh. He was so surprised that he could not maintain his composure and so began to laugh out loud for the longest time.

Shortly thereafter, she excused herself and closed the door. John sat on the last step of the stairwell and laughed until his diaphragm was sore and tight.

"Well, I guess he doesn't live there anymore," he spoke out loud in English as he began to hop down the stairs. He needed a plan now. First, to the restaurant, to find his friend, and then to contact his wife and children. By now, there was probably some sort of missing person report, and the police would be crawling all over looking for him. As he headed to the restaurant, he stopped in an internet café to check his email and see if there was any news of his abduction. He paid the clerk for 30 minutes, found a computer, and logged into the World Wide Web. He went to a local news station's website and searched for any headline that might tell him about his own kidnapping. He stumbled on a headline not on the local news website but on CNN's national website that told of a Dentist's ransom and subsequent execution.

The story was that the dentist had been taken by a terrorist organization, who had contacted the family demanding a large sum of money. Apparently, he came from a rather well-connected family (as the story said). When the payout was late, they took him to a bridge and drove him in, car and all. He sat motionless in front of the bright screen, staring at the photo of himself and a picture of his dental office. It was the strangest feeling he had ever experienced. There was his little Honda being towed out of the Missouri River and a host of photos of the crime scene where his blood and DNA were purported to have been found all over the inside of the car. Again, he sat without any idea what to think, staring at the millions of tiny pixels on the large LCD screen. He scrolled through the photos of the crime scene, looking for any information that he might use. Suddenly, his family popped into his head. If they thought he was dead…He had to call them, he thought, and a sense of true urgency began to build from deep within his heart.

He had known that he needed to make contact with his wife and children to make sure that they were all okay and that they knew he was okay, but with this latest development of his apparent murder, he wasn't sure what to do. Should he contact them and dispel the false murder? Probably not was the answer, as if he did contact his wife, the people who did this to him (or created the illusion that they did this to him) would most likely be aware and take out their frustrations on his family. He was deathly frightened at that moment. His wife thought he was dead. His parents and all of his friends also thought he was dead. Most likely, his office manager had notified all of his patients that he was dead and had tried to contact someone to cover for him and take care of the enormous debt that still hung over the practice. "Wow," he thought, "what was he going to do?"

There he was, in the corner of a little computer café, closed off to the world around him, a man who apparently did not exist, who was hunted, no doubt by terrorists, and would not be long for the world unless he could do something, something that would remedy the situation…

He placed his hands behind his head and leaned back in the chair as far as it would go without banging into the glass door separating him from the other cubicles occupied by engaged occupants. Quieting his mind, he tried to focus on what was happening.

His mind raced back to a time many years ago... he remembered the bleak and dreary morning when he and Elder Walker were out on their bicycles, traveling to an appointment. They turned a corner and came across the most gut-wrenching and outright bizarre sight either of them had ever seen. A pedestrian had been hit by a van, and the man lay in the middle of the street, obviously in some agony and pain. The driver of the van had stepped out and was trying to ascertain the pedestrian's condition. What happened next was strange. The driver went back to the van and returned with a large white sheet, which he unfolded and placed over the severely injured pedestrian. The injured man began to scream in pain, and the driver started shouting at him. Here was a man lying critically injured in the middle of the street, and the driver was shouting at him. Then, silence. The man lay still, motionless in the street, the white sheet now blood-soaked. Silence. Silence like none the two missionaries had ever seen. It seemed as though the silence had descended upon them and their surroundings like a fog, silent and immovable, like mist on the ocean.

He sat quietly, lost in his thoughts, when he heard—or rather, felt—the air grow suddenly tense with suspense. Once again, he perceived all that was happening around him simultaneously. Even with his eyes closed and his back to the front of the store, he could sense the presence of someone who sought to harm him. After a moment or two, it became clear that he was not free, and definitely, he did not have a long life expectancy. He could feel the man moving into the café, and he sensed the presence of the weapon the man bore. The metal was a cold and unforgiving mass as it was hoisted from the leather underarm holster and brought to bear, still concealed within the dark business suit.

Almost instinctively, John reached down into his backpack and withdrew the handgun he had been carrying for the past 36 hours. He felt himself release the safety as he brought it up with the bag and placed it on his lap, his hand on the grip, finger on the trigger. He had attached the silencer the previous evening after finding it in the pile of things he had stolen from his captors and dropped into his backpack, thinking it might be wise to avoid drawing attention to himself if the unthinkable should happen and he needed to use the firearm he had also absconded with.

Eyes open, he watched as the unknown man approached his booth, preparing to strike with so many ounces of lead thrown at so many thousand feet per second... As soon as the man opened the door, there were three light but audible taps with accompanying puffs of smoke. John's eyes widened as he saw the man take two more steps toward him before stopping and beginning to fall. Smoke rose quickly from the backpack on John's lap. John immediately stood and braced the man to avoid a clamorous landing, directing him into the seat John had been occupying. He propped him up slightly, then surveyed the crowd for any signs of awareness. Shocked, he stood silently for a moment, then looked about one more time. Fortunately for him, the combination of apathy and soundproof glass gave him the all-clear signal.

He made a swift exit, running out of the store, making a right toward his stolen moped, only to collide headfirst with another large, dark-skinned man. Unfortunately, this man was prepared for him and hit him squarely on the back of the head as he turned to run, inducing instantaneous unconsciousness.

Chapter 16
A Near-Death Experience

Although he didn't die, he came within just a few seconds of his death. The nitro pills took effect at the very last moment possible. One more microsecond and Wen Zhang would have died. As it happened, he sat up, clutching his chest and screaming obscenities. He managed to catch his breath and cough a few more times before he was able to fully function.

The trucks had gone, and the workers had disappeared as well. He found himself alone in the loading dock, with only $20,000 and a picture of his family, his beloved family. His once stone-cold heart began to melt, and a solitary tear rolled down his cheek. He hated himself and loathed the man he once was, the one who destroyed everything wonderful about his family. Yet, he still loved them and needed them more than he could admit. He put his head down and sobbed for a few minutes before regaining his composure. Feeling a pang of urgency, he dialed his ex-wife's phone number.

She answered the phone, and he began the conversation he had avoided for almost 20 years. They talked for nearly an hour about the children and their regrets of the past. Wen Zhang tried to help her understand his feelings for her, for their children, and his hatred for what he had done in the past, along with his never-ending guilt and pain. He shared the agreements he had made and the actions he had set in motion, assuring her that he was going to make it right. When he hung up, he left her shocked and in tears.

He was going to make it right. He didn't know how, and he wasn't sure if he would survive it, but he would make this right.

He dialed information and began the search for the man he had once known, who was in the CIA.

Rummaging through the briefcase that he had retrieved from the trunk of his car, he finally found the number of a man he had met in Dubai. "Nice man," he thought, "although a bit rough around the edges." Wen Zhang wasn't quite sure about the man's background, but he was certain that he was heavily involved with the CIA, and he was really the only one with intelligence connections that he knew.

Picking up the phone from the desk in front of him, he dialed the international code, and then the phone number for the man he thought could help. The line rang exactly three times, and then Charles answered.

Wen Zhang choked a little bit before finally introducing himself and explaining the situation that he was into his friend. He revealed everything, feeling rather desperate and having no one else to turn to, so he spilled all the beans.

Charles was silent for a long few moments as he digested the information from his would-be friend. His reply was terse and abrupt. "I am in Taichung; where would you like to meet?"

Wen Zhang suddenly had a sinking feeling deep in the pit of his stomach and hung up without any more thought. In Taiwan? How was he in Taiwan? The last time he spoke with Charles, he was stationed in Dubai, investigating the smuggling of hazardous biological waste products.

He gathered all that he had with him and hopped back into his car, speeding off toward his home office. He needed to contact the family of the man he had doomed to death. He needed to remedy the death warrant he had issued and fix the nightmare he had created.

Sitting in his car, waiting at the stoplight, he saw the man he had just spoken with on the phone—Charles, the agent—in a Lexus behind him. What? His heart began to pound, and the sting returned, as it had prior to the heart attack he had just endured a few moments ago.

He floored the gas pedal the moment the light changed and was home in moments. He pulled into the garage and watched as the automatic door closed, shutting out his pursuer.

He took the elevator up to the 73rd floor, holding his chest the whole time. The heat was intense now, more so than before. He began to step out of the elevator and only made it three steps before he collapsed to the floor, doubled over in agony. He could not breathe now, and the sting felt like a small razor was slowly dissecting his chest, opening his heart one agonizingly painful slice at a time. He lay there, panting shallow breaths, one after another.

After a few moments, he managed to crawl into his office, where he re-accessed the name he had given to the terrorists. He dialed the phone number as his heart began to pound slowly. He could count the beats; now, it was less than one per second. The ringing suddenly stopped, and a young woman's voice answered.

———

John awoke with a headache unlike any he had ever felt before. The back of his neck and the lower part of his skull throbbed with a pulsating ache, bordering on jackhammering. He found himself blindfolded, lying on the floor of a van. He could hear the vehicle driving down what sounded like a dirt road, a very rough dirt road. He could hear some voices in the front of the van talking about something in a language other than English or Chinese. After a long drive and what seemed like a billion bumps, large and small, the van stopped. John was manhandled into another vehicle, and his blindfold was forcefully removed. He was inside a plane now, a small private leer-type jet. He was escorted to the back of the jet, and his bonds were cut. He sat down in the plush oversized leather chair and surveyed his captors. There were four men in total, including the pilot, and they were all seemingly different in nationality and skin color.

They sat in silence, captor and captive, for the longest time. Finally, one of them spoke. He appeared Taiwanese, though he could have been Chinese. The conversation, if you could call it that, was completely one-sided, more a barking of orders and roaring threats than a dialogue.

The plan was this: John, who was now officially dead to the rest of the world, was to deliver a payment to a location they would designate later. He was to make the delivery to their contact, take a picture of the contact with the briefcase, and send it back to the terrorists. In exchange, they promised not to harm his family. John sat aghast. He could hardly fathom the thought of his family being held hostage: his little girls, his wife, frightened and imprisoned... His heart began to race, and he suddenly started sweating. The man continued in a calm voice, stating that they had plenty of leverage to ensure he delivered the package. He reached inside his jacket and pulled out a series of photographs of John's wife and children, apparently taken while they were playing at the city park near their home in suburban Kansas City. John's heart sank deep into his stomach. He wanted to lash out and kill the men who held him prisoner and threatened his wife and children. Rage began to build from deep within him, a power he had never felt before. Again, the oriental spoke in his broken English.

"It's only a delivery of payment. You make the delivery, you are free to go. Your family will be glad to see you." John leaped to his feet in a sheer uncontrollable rage and jumped toward the little man. His only thought was to break free and be with his family. He was only able to grasp the terrorist's shoulders before feeling the long syringe hit his leg. Within a few seconds, his eyesight began to fail, and his arms became totally numb. He could feel the wave of the paralytic agent ascend from his leg to his abdomen, then to his arms. He fell to the floor and watched as the men above him laughed while he slowly lost consciousness, fading into complete submissiveness and utter darkness.

Chapter 17
Do You Not Know?

She listened for only a few moments to the silent phone before reaching for the end call button. Just as she moved to hang up, the man on the other end spoke. His heavily accented English was spoken slowly yet clearly.

"Is Doctor Campbell there?" the voice asked, and the woman began to cry.

"What?" she asked. "Do you not know?" she queried.

He thought for a moment and then asked, "Not know what?"

She choked a bit and sobbed slightly as she told him of the scene at the bridge. Then she could bear it no more and hung up the phone.

Wen Zhang sat in amazement in his apartment, staring at the phone. He remained on the floor, unable to move, paralyzed by the magnitude of the pain he was experiencing. He wasn't sure which was causing more anguish: the news that he had sent an innocent man to his death or the pain in his failing heart.

He again clutched his chest, trying to breathe, attempting to force the oxygenated blood through his arteries, but he could not overcome the pain. He was helpless against the utter magnitude and depth of the pain. Unable to breathe, he slumped into the corner and began to pound on the floor. Slowly, his consciousness faded; his arm became weak, and he began to relax. He couldn't tell if he was dying or if he had just shot up like before. His brain had released the final stockpile of pain-eliminating endorphins, and he felt wonderful, but just for a minute. He turned to his left the moment he heard the buzzing sound, only to see nothing. Nothing but blackness. His eyesight failed him, and he sat motionless on the floor. He began to feel an overpowering sense of guilt. All he felt was guilt, paralyzing guilt. All of his transgressions and shortcomings were at once laid bare. He sighed deeply. His chest heaved once, a great gasp for air, and then held still, locked in a permanent state of catatonic agony.

―――――

Jamison had been notified of the shooting at the internet café and had arrived, posing as a local tourist drawn to the commotion. Although he arrived several hours after the event, he was able to ascertain what had happened from the crowd and a few witnesses who were questioned at the scene.

Apparently, another American had left just before this man was found dead in the computer cubicle. The police had no idea who either of the men were, as there was no ID on the dead man, and no one really knew who the American was. Jamison waited for the crowd and the police to disperse before heading up to the café clerk to ask a couple of questions, this time posing as a friend of the first American. The clerk was altogether unhelpful but did mention that he remembered swiping a credit card of the first American. Jamison convinced him to look up the number and the name and was not astounded to hear that the man was, in reality, the dentist from Kansas City he had spoken with that very same morning.

As of yet, there was no connection made connecting the dentist to the terrorist cell and the shooting, but Jamison was going to make that happen very quickly as soon as he discovered the identity of the decedent.

He headed to his hotel and ran an image search program to try to identify the man whose photo he had taken with his camera phone as the police carted the corpse away. After several hours of scanning photos and eliminating possibilities, the name of the man popped up on the screen. This man was very high up in the organization, apparently either second or third in command to al-Akezemi. If this man was out of commission, there would be a shakeup in the hierarchy and perhaps a blunder in the execution of the attack.

Jamison immediately phoned into central command and shared the information with his handler. However, he was ignored almost completely and was informed that the agency had its eyes on a cargo plane that was to land in San Francisco that afternoon. The agency had credible intel that the nuclear threat was on board that plane. All resources were diverted to counter the possible nuclear threat. The plane had departed Taiwan under Jamison's watch. He was as good as a desk jockey now; the handler had berated him before hanging up on him.

Jamison sat on the uncomfortable chair, staring at his computer, wondering how he had gone so wrong. He had missed the transaction and let the nuclear device out of Taiwan, all completely unaware of what was going on. Frustrated and angry, he stood, picked up the small chair he was sitting on, and threw it into a wall opposite the desk. After a few swear words, he was feeling quite a bit better, so he sat on the bed, thinking. He made a call and activated a trace on the credit card number the clerk at the internet café had given him, just in case Dr. Campbell showed up anywhere. The moment the card was swiped, if it was ever swiped again, he would know. Just as he was digging into a hearty steak from room service, his phone rang. It was the agent in Kansas City whom Jamison had asked to watch Dr. Campbell.

"They killed him, Jamison. They took him and ran him off a bridge. They killed him," the agent exclaimed urgently.

"What?" Jamison thought. He asked the agent what he meant, and the agent explained the information about the bridge and the car and the DNA they matched to the dentist found on the scene. Jamison explained to him that it was impossible because the dentist was in Taiwan this morning. Just several hours ago, they had met and talked.

Perplexed and unsatisfied with the new information, Jamison turned to his steak.

———

He awoke in a car, in the back seat, still bound and gagged from the flight. He couldn't remember how they had cleared customs or the airport or anything like that, but he was sure that some homeland security protocol had been grossly violated. What, in reality, happened was that there was a huge security alert, and the entire nation was raised to whatever threat level was needed. All the inbound planes en route to LAX had been rerouted to alternate airports, but some had been able to continue on to land. The plane the dentist had been on just happened to be a government plane from the People's Republic of Taiwan, which had a diplomatic pass through some of the security clearances.

The terrorists had evacuated the plane on the runway, dragged their drugged hostage into a limousine, and begun the drive from California to Kansas City. Shortly after the limousine left the airport, the terrorists had called in a bomb threat, identifying a certain cargo plane. The agency and local law enforcement shut down the entire airport and the surrounding city, evacuating anyone close enough to feel nuclear fallout.

All the police in the state of California were on alert due to that one matter, and hence, the roads were nearly totally free of speed traps. The limousine traveled unimpeded across the United States, taking only breaks for restroom stops and refueling. They had an impressively good time as they traversed the West, the Rocky Mountains, and the plains. Throughout the entire trip, John was drugged in the back of the limo and forced to pee into a jar when he did wake up enough to realize he had to go. Fading in and out of consciousness, he had the most vivid collage of dreams and images flash through his mind. It seemed that the sedative drug he had been given was a means to unlock a flood of images, memories, and recollections from his past, most of which were not the most pleasant.

―――――

Chapter 18
Road Trip

The first series of images began with his experience in dental school. He could see himself sitting in the orientation room, listening to the various administrators talk about the program, the future, the expectations, and the challenges. He remembered the sheer excitement he felt as he woke up on the first day of dental school, anticipating the day's happenings. He recalled the many labs he experienced in his first year and the smell of methyl methacrylate monomer that often filled the entire school on denture lab days.

His mind continued to drift into half-sleep as the limo droned down the interstate, finally resting on his first patient, his first day in the clinic. He visualized walking out to the waiting room and calling the name of the patient. He could feel the nerves inside him tense and relax, tense and relax, as he relived that experience. He recalled the first night following his first assignment in oral surgery when he awoke in a panic, nervous that he had extracted the wrong tooth from his first extraction patient.

His mind fought with the challenges he had experienced during his formative years in dental school, trying over and over to find congruence in balancing study, work, family, and clinic. He remembered the times he had sacrificed his study time for his children and how his GPA had suffered as a result. He recalled the stress from school and the constant nagging desire to apply to a specialty program, which slowly dissolved his ability to think clearly and deal with life's stressors. The next image was that of a family vacation over Christmas break after his first semester in school. He had called the grade line to find out what his semester GPA and accompanying grades were. He was in the back of a 15-passenger van with his wife, two kids, and a host of other relatives, driving from one attraction to another when he made the call. He listened intently as the automated voice chanted the title of the class and the section of the class and then spoke the grade for each respective class.

His heart sank as he relived the memory, and the mechanical voice reiterated the less-than-outstanding grades—at least, less than outstanding for someone who wanted to apply to a specialist program. He had about a 3.5 after the first semester, and it was devastatingly depressing. He knew that to apply to specialty programs, he needed nearly a perfect GPA, and 3.5 was not going to cut it. He sat in the seat with his kids climbing on him, the weight of the world on his shoulders, and his dreams slowly fading into oblivion. He fell into a relative depression at that moment, not quite able to cope with his own lack of achievement and the seeming closing of those future doors of possibility. His mind changed, his thoughts darkened slightly, and his demeanor faltered. Certain aspects of his life began to unravel, and his self-image shifted dramatically. He had to accept that he was going to be just a normal person and nothing more. The depression returned as John lay in the limo, bouncing slightly as it turned into a gas station.

The next image was that of sheer darkness. John was startled at the darkness that came into his mind. It was not a blackness of thought or image but rather a complete lack of any images. His mind rewound a bit to the initiation of his depression, then replayed the next few moments, only to become stuck in the void of memory again. Rousing slightly with the strain of focusing, he deliberately tried to force himself to remember, to recall and relive what had happened thereafter. He tried and tried, bearing down on his mind, attempting to coerce the memory to resurface. No success. That memory had been buried.

The limo stopped at the gas station, and the driver and two of the occupants hopped out to get some refreshments and use the restroom while the third man filled the gas tank and kept an eye on the captive. John immediately awakened from his half-sleep when the door was closed after the third man exited the limo. He did not stir but rather tried to get his bearings and determine where he was. Realizing that he was alone in the heavily tinted limo, he sat up and tried to untie his hands and feet. The bonds were so knotted that it would take a knife or a lot of time, neither of which he currently had at his disposal. He began searching for something, some instrument, something sharp to cut free his hands and ankles. As his eyes swept the interior of the car, he saw a map that had fallen to the floor and was partially covered in coffee stains. He immediately recognized the map as a map of the US and followed the highlighted interstate line straight from LA to KC.

He immediately spoke, "Why are they taking me back to KC?" and was shocked to hear himself speak out loud after nearly 20 hours of half-sleep. He continued to look around, and his eyes came to rest on a briefcase, an old leather briefcase. There was something familiar about that briefcase; he wasn't sure what it was. There was a suit hanging from one of the garment hooks near the front of the passenger cabin and a bunch of garbage consisting mostly of wrappers and magazines strewn throughout the car. Like a clap of thunder, the briefcase popped back into his mind, along with the first time he saw it. It was the case that he had seen sitting on the table in the apartment in Taiwan! He looked back at the case and immediately knew that it was indeed the same case. It seemed, though, that it was not quite closed all the way; perhaps something was wedged in it, keeping it slightly open, although it had been forced shut and latched. John squinted a bit through the haze of his grogginess and saw what looked like wires, two of them twisted around each other, with a short loop about half an inch long sticking out of the side of the case, keeping it open just a bit.

He recalled the conversation he had with Jamison and the words "nuclear threat." His mind began to swirl, and his heart raced. He looked up through the tinted glass just in time to see the third man recap the gasoline tank and run inside to pay in cash. John's mind began to smoke as he ran through every possible scenario for escape. As he did this, he realized that he could hear the men coming. Barely in time, he lay down and did his best to reassume the sleeping position he had been in prior to waking up. The three men reentered the vehicle, and they were soon on their way east across the flat and desolate Kansas to their destination. John listened for everything he possibly could as the men chatted in some foreign language he couldn't understand. His interest was piqued as he heard the words "NASCAR" and "message." John immediately felt that he knew precisely what was going on. He understood that the men wanted him to think he was bringing a briefcase of money to the stadium to give to a certain contact so his family would no longer be under threat. But he also understood that if he brought that briefcase to the stadium, the results would be disastrous.

John knew little to nothing about nuclear weapons. Aside from the fact that a comparatively small device, if armed with the right explosives and mechanism, could create an enormously powerful and destructive blast of nuclear energy, he had no technical understanding of nuclear devices. The consequence of a wrong move or tampering with the device could prove disastrous. He lay in mental anguish, knowing that he somehow held the lives of more than a hundred thousand people in his hands. Not only the people who were at the NASCAR race within the stadium and the surrounding RV encampment but also the adjacent town of Bonner Springs and all of the populous of eastern Kansas and western Missouri could be affected by a blast, not to mention the radioactive fallout that would rain down for weeks all across the entire Midwest. John was nearly frantic when he suddenly remembered the comment made by his Organic Chemistry professor, Dr. Holder, that nuclear weapons required a very specific detonation mechanism and that you could probably take a sledgehammer to the side of a nuclear warhead and it wouldn't detonate unless intentionally triggered.

With his newfound hope, he determined that he would wait for the right moment to attempt to disarm the weapon. He would contact law enforcement if possible, maybe some sort of bomb squad. But if that was not an option, he would have to make a go at it himself. Even if perhaps the weapon was guarded by some sort of failsafe, it would be better for it to detonate away from the stadium rather than in the middle of a densely packed sporting event.

Just then, the limo hit a large bump as it trundled along down the freeway at 90 miles per hour. John has bounced nearly completely around, facing toward the center of the cabin rather than away. The men made no notice of his new position as they, too, were recovering from their own jostling about. John carefully peered through one eye to determine if he was safe to look about a bit. Two of the men sat in the front seat, one driving, one in the passenger seat, and the third man was asleep himself in the back seat with his feet up. John carefully looked about and relocated the briefcase. He also saw his backpack and, upon the discovery, remembered all that he had in that backpack. He had a weapon (if the men had not removed it), a large hunting knife, and a bunch of dental anesthetic with accompanying syringes and needles. He wasn't sure why he had brought the dental anesthetic with him, but he had just felt as if he should grab it on his way out of the office before he left on this wild adventure.

Chapter 19
Who Would Have Been Calling from Taiwan?

John's wife sat in anguish after throwing the phone on the floor. She was in a state of hopelessness and depression after hearing from Detective Dibbens that her husband and the father of their children had been killed. He had mentioned to her that the car had been so destroyed by the accident and the crash off of the bridge into the river that, most likely, there would not be a conventional funeral, and she should consider a closed casket. The comment had made her angry, and she lashed out at the incompetent detective, berating him for not keeping a closer watch on her husband. She had angrily told him to leave and then slammed the door, retiring to the couch to sob. She was only there for a few moments when the phone rang again.

She had dropped her children off at her mother's house as she dug through the piles of paper and files in her husband's desk in the basement, looking for his life insurance policies. She was angry at him for leaving her and felt victimized by this war on terror that had gone on for so long. The life insurance agent had phoned previously, asking her to find the policies so they could make the funeral and the mess afterward as quick and painless as possible. "Painless," she thought, "painless?"

She loved the children and wasn't sure how to tell them about their daddy. He was a good daddy and spent as much time as he thought he could with his kiddies. They were very close to him and often would cry when he would leave for work in the morning or after lunch. "It was going to break their little hearts," she thought to herself. Again, deep sobbing. She didn't know what else to do. She cried. After some concerted effort searching in the basement, she happened upon the life insurance policies. She counted them and then added the totals. After settling the debts with the bank on the dental practice, the home, and his remaining student loans, she would have a little bit of money left to save and invest. It seemed to be just enough to live on without ever having to work until the kids were all in school.

That's not what she wanted, though. She was happy, at least up until about three days ago when her whole life went sideways. She walked up the stairs and sat down on the couch again. Her mind slipped back a few weeks to her discovering her husband's journal and the surprises she had come across. Normally, she was not the type to dig into someone's personal life, but at that time, she had noticed that her husband had been doing a lot of writing in his notebook, and she had just a bit of curiosity. She thought perhaps that his life was hiding something, something that she needed to know. She had been cleaning the bedroom and picked it up off of the floor from under the bed where he usually dropped it with his scriptures in the evening and had opened it just out of pure, innocent curiosity.

The journal was only about six months old, and as she scanned through the pages, her image of the man she married suddenly began to change.

Granted, he had his moments and was at times reserved, borderline depressed, and pretty stressed out, but this life that his journal described was a different man altogether. He spoke of his recollections on starting his business and how, at times, he was so exasperated with the stress and the pressure that he felt like his life would slide into oblivion. He spoke of how many of his previous choices had given him a great deal of remorse and guilt and that he carried that every day. His life was a concatenation of images singed with the flame of hindsight's disdain. This man who wrote this journal had great regret, incredible stress, and yet a great deal of hope. It seemed, as she read that every time he would talk about the many instances of unrelenting pressure and stress, shortly thereafter, he would find hope and faith in the guidance he sought.

It was amazing. She did not know this man. He was familiar, but at the same time, he was only a vestige of the man she knew. Repeatedly, she encountered resolute statements of how he felt like the only reason he could and would be able to deal with the challenges and stresses on a daily basis was with the knowledge that his family and his little children relied completely on him. He could not afford any mental breakdowns or egregious errors that would disrupt his little family. She was astounded at the level of hardships and stumbling blocks that he suffered through. For a moment, she thought there might be some evidence of weakness or discretion but found exactly the opposite. She thought to herself that she must have had her eyes shut pretty tight to miss his pain and challenges. They were not shut, she realized, just focused on the little persons she was so faithfully trying to raise. She also stumbled upon a section of his journal where he described his connection with her, his need to be with her, and how tightly bound his emotions and feelings were to hers. He spoke of how he tried to be a better man to make her life easier when she was down but mentioned that it was so very difficult to overcome the congruent emotional connection. Last of all, he spoke of how much he needed her and loved her. She had cried most of the afternoon after reading that passage.

She did not tell him that she had read his journal, although she suspected he might have known.

She sat on the couch, reliving those moments, and the thought of the phone call from Taiwan popped into her mind. "Who could have been calling from Taiwan?" she wondered.

John had been working on the knots for a good hour now while the man in the back of the car slept. The two men in the front of the car had closed the privacy window, and it sounded like they had music on. Periodically, they would hit a bump or pass a truck, causing the man in the back to open his eyes for a moment just to make sure all was well. Finally, he worked his hands free. He first reached for his bag, which was sitting about 4 feet away. After carefully maneuvering himself and sliding slightly on the chair, he was able to get hold of it and slowly slide it toward him. He felt through the front pocket for his knife, the one he had purchased on his honeymoon in Yellowstone National Park, and soon found it nestled up against the outside mesh pocket. Slowly unzipping the zipper one tooth at a time, he opened enough space to wiggle his hand into the bag's smaller front pocket and locate the knife. He opened it inside the bag, just in case the latch clicked; the bag might afford some degree of soundproofing. Withdrawing the knife, he headed for the briefcase and the exposed wires.

He thought that the safest bet would be to cut both ends of the loop dangling out of the bag, so that there would be no free end to draw attention to the fact that the bomb had been disarmed. If, in fact, it had actually been disarmed. There was a chance that the men had installed some sort of failsafe to detonate the bomb in case of tampering. All the same, John proceeded, either stupidly or bravely.

He pulled the loop taut with the index finger of his left hand and began working on the upper loop with the knife in his right hand. Cutting through the first loop of wires proved very easy, and the car didn't even explode in a nuclear fireball, either. The wires were of fairly small gauge, the kind the Dentist imagined would connect the control mechanism to the actual detonator.

The second end of the loop proved a bit more hazardous. Just as he pressed the knife against the loop, the driver of the car careened to avoid an obstacle on the road, and the blade deeply lacerated John's finger. The man in the back of the car fell off the seat and onto the floor, thrashing about wildly.

John's eyes met the other man's just as the knife blade bit into his finger. The terrorist lunged at him, and John immediately brought the knife to bear. It was only a 4-inch hunting knife, but it saved John's life. After steadying himself, the man jumped toward John, who was about 4 feet away. As the man's hands found John's neck, the blade of the knife slipped effortlessly through the terrorist's ribs, piercing his heart. Even a trained surgeon couldn't have caused more damage. The blade slid into the left ventricle, opening a 3cm laceration in the heart muscle wall, and the man immediately went into cardiac arrest. His fingers lost their grip around John's neck, and his blood poured all over John, who was still tied together at the ankles. John never screamed or yelped, only gasped as he pulled the knife from the terrorist's chest before rolling onto the floor again.

John sat up, grabbed the knife from the dead man's hands, and quickly freed himself. He thought for sure that the men in the front of the limo would soon open the sliding window to make sure that all was well and that there were no incidents with the swerving. He hurriedly grabbed his bag and searched the man for a cell phone, wallet, or weapon. He found a semi-auto handgun and a cell phone. Upon finding the cell phone, he dialed 911.

He spoke softly but was very precise, not allowing the operator on the other end to ask any questions, as he thought he had only seconds before being discovered. As he was explaining the situation, he looked up to see that they were nearing the end of the Kansas Turnpike and were only moments from the stadium he knew all too well. Panic set in, and he dropped the phone just as he was getting to the explanation of the bomb. When the phone hit the floor, the battery pack popped off, ending the call. John looked up at the glass to see if there was any way to lock the glass window closed. He pressed the button labeled "privacy" and then sat back and thought for a moment, looking up at the glass window.

He was traveling at 90 mph in a limo with three terrorists, one of whom was dead, and a disarmed nuclear bomb. He was covered in blood and exposed to who knows what infectious diseases. He breathed a sigh of relief thinking about the bomb and picked up the case to make sure there were no other wires he should venture to cut. There was no combination, so he directly clicked open the latches. Opening the case, he discovered, to his utmost shock, that there was a cell phone attached to what looked like a PDA, glued to a fat aluminum thermos bottle that was about 6 inches in diameter. The green wires he had sliced were just extra wires stuffed in next to the device. Suddenly, the cell phone rang—a high-pitched ring reminiscent of the older, larger cell phones of yesteryear. After ringing, the cell phone chirped again, and then the PDA attached to the thermos blinked brightly. The screen displayed some sort of Cyrillic or Arabic, then began to count down in seconds from 30 minutes. John suddenly began to panic, thinking he would meet his maker in less than 30 minutes.

As the car drove on toward its destination, a crowded sports arena, John inspected the device closely. The metal housing was most likely stainless steel, with the top and bottom of the metal cylinder spot-welded onto the main body. It looked like one of those expensive coffee thermos mugs you get when you spend thirty thousand dollars on a car. Whoever made this device knew it would need to be sealed and welded to avoid any second thoughts by the delivering party. John thought that if he could just remove the cell phone and the PDA, perhaps the device would disarm. He took the cell phone and easily broke it off; it was only superglued on. There were no wires connecting the cell phone to the PDA or the thermos.

"What?" he thought, "How is that possible?" He sat in amazement as the blood began to dry and become sticky on his shirt, wondering what this was. "Was this all some sort of elaborate joke? How could it possibly be a bomb," he thought. He set the case down on the seat and then picked up the thermos with its accompanying PDA. There was a small icon on the PDA screen that looked like a speaker, and John decided to try and turn off the bomb with the PDA. He pressed the screen and tried to activate the menu functions with no success. This was a Dell PDA, one of the best and most expensive, equipped with Bluetooth and Wi-Fi—it could do anything and everything. Apparently, this particular PDA had some very specific software installed. He was sure that someone could hack it, but not in 21 minutes. The screen had no options, only the timer and a speaker icon. When John pressed the speaker icon, the PDA screen blinked again, and a beeping sound, consistent with one beep per second, began. "Dang," John thought, "what now?"

———

Chapter 20
Where's My Watch?

Just then, the driver or passenger began to bang on the glass, trying to get the dead terrorist to open up. John banged back in haste, and the banging apparently appeased the men in the front as they stopped banging altogether. Suddenly, a sharp turn and John could see that he was no longer on the interstate but rather heading toward the speedway, which he could see about 1 mile away. He looked at the time on the PDA. 20:05 and counting down, beeping all the while. He angrily pried at the PDA and cracked the screen, but it still beeped. He broke through the cyanoacrylate bond and tore the plastic housing of the PDA off the metal canister. No wires anywhere. He bashed the PDA on the floor and kicked the screen repeatedly. The screen went dim, but the beeping did not relent.

To his horror, the beeping was coming from inside the canister. It had been emanating from the canister the whole time it had been activated. The PDA must have triggered the mechanism via Bluetooth, WiFi, or radio frequency. "Oh no!" he thought. "Where's my watch? I have no watch...." Quickly calculating how many seconds were in 18 minutes, he began to count backward from 1140. After a few seconds, the limo turned down the service entrance to the speedway, and John suddenly noticed the fleet of police cars in pursuit of them. Several cars ahead had cops waiting, guns drawn, forming a roadblock. Perhaps his 911 call had worked. But worked for what? No one could disarm a welded nuclear canister in 1090 seconds! He needed to open the canister; he needed to break these welds. He was sure there was some other device nestled snugly up to the nuclear fuel that could be unplugged or cut or something to stop this horrific scene. He continued counting downward as he reached for his pocket knife. He wedged the blade into one of the spaces between the welds and tried to pry the lid off. The blade broke off about 6mm, and he angrily threw it to the floor, the 6mm tip still wedged tightly in the gap between the welded lid and cylinder.

———————

Just then, John heard the first gunshots, followed by the ensuing pings and bangs as the rounds embedded themselves in the vehicle. The driver accelerated through the roadblock, bashing through the two police cars centered in the road. Badly damaged, with occupants thrown about, the car continued under the raceway and up into the center of the track. With 1050 seconds left, the driver pulled onto the raceway and headed past the pit toward the west seating area. John could see the shock on the faces of many onlookers as they watched a shot-up and beat-up limousine blast through a police roadblock and speed onto a high-speed racetrack. All of the stock cars managed to avoid the limo as it careened wildly toward the man charged with waving the flags, signaling the drivers. The car came to a terrific halt as it crashed into the concrete wall separating the track from the crowd just beneath the flag man, with 15 police cars in tow. Instantly, the police surrounded the limo, and the drivers were pulled from the car. John could see that the passenger was badly injured from the crash and what also looked like several gunshot wounds to the chest and face. John's door was opened, and he was dragged out of the car by several police officers, one on each limb. He was commanded to drop the canister, and he quickly shouted at the top of his lungs that it was a nuclear bomb. Immediately, the crowd went deathly silent. The beeping became readily apparent to the officers who were close to John.

Astounded, the police had no idea what to do. Quickly, John explained that the bomb would detonate within 15 minutes and that he needed to get as far away as possible to save the lives of as many people as possible. As he said it, he was already moving toward one of the stock cars. Surprisingly, the police allowed him to do so, appearing completely unprepared for the situation or, more likely, understanding that a well-maintained NASCAR would likely be the best way of transporting the nuclear device as far away as quickly as possible. John could see the looks in many of their eyes as they comprehended the sincerity of his statement.

The driver moved out of the car and began to run. John tossed the beeping steel cylinder into the car and slid in through the window. He had driven one of these cars before, and it was a graduation gift when he graduated from dental school. His father-in-law had taken him for a morning at the raceway. The experience had been exhilarating—600 horsepower, 200 miles per hour. Who wouldn't want to?

Aside from being in the arms of his loving wife and children, he couldn't think of a better way to die than driving 200 miles per hour down Interstate 70. As he moved into the car, fighting back sobs and tears, he yelled to one of the police to have the interstate west of Bonner Springs cleared and to let the cops know he was on a mission to save the world. He started the engine and moved the car out of the stadium and onto the interstate, accelerating as fast as he possibly could. The suspension of the car had been specially tuned for the unique banking of the raceway, so it was a constant battle to keep the car going straight.

He made it up to about 200 mph when it finally dawned on him that he could probably open the case. There may only be one way, and he would likely only get one shot at it, though. Just as the realization hit him, he realized he had lost count of where the bomb countdown was. Slamming on the brakes, he almost lost control of the car. He screeched off the exit ramp and toward Bonner Springs, bringing to bear all of the 600 horsepower in that finely tuned racing engine. Still covered in now-dried blood, with tears pouring down his face, he thought only of his wife and his children as he blazed down the highway at 200 mph. He could see their faces at the window; he could hear them begging him to chase them or swing them in the blanket.

Faith, he thought to himself; have faith. He couldn't die, he thought, he just couldn't die.

Turning the corner and blowing the red light, he pulled into the strip mall and parked immediately in front of the dental office where he had first started after dental school. He grabbed the canister and slid out of the car window, leaving it to roll slightly back toward the grassy embankment.

The office was open, and the patients and front office team were completely surprised to see a man covered in the blood come bursting through the door. He said nothing to anyone. He didn't have the strength to speak. Every ounce of energy and focus he had was devoted to one thing and one thing only: living for his young family. He went into the nearest dental operatory and sat down at the doctor's chair, lifting the handpiece and placing a new 1557 bur from the bur box that was kept in the top drawer into the chuck of the drill. Two of the dental assistants recognized him from several years ago but were too appalled by his blood-covered appearance to say anything to him. He began to drill through the spot welds on the canister one by one, with air and water spraying everywhere.

He had to change the bur several times as the stainless steel and whatever metal was used in the welding would break the carbide bur tips after only a short amount of drilling. Spinning at nearly four hundred thousand revolutions per minute, the drilling eventually took care of all of the welds; the dentist dropped the handpiece immediately after the last weld was cut. He hurriedly unscrewed the cylinder top that was free-spinning now and pulled off the lid, tossing it to the floor.

Looking inside, he saw another smaller device, some sort of modified cell phone mechanism attached to the small cuboidal-shaped thing, which he assumed to be the bomb. Tears streaking down his cheeks, blood covering his arms and chest, he gripped the customized cell phone and quickly pulled it out of the canister. His left index finger throbbed more now than before from the previous knife laceration, but he managed to extract the innards of the bomb. There was yet one more set of green wires, which he pulled on to separate from their connections to the bomb. The beeping immediately stopped.

John set the dismantled makings of a small nuclear device in the dental chair, placed his head in his hands, and started to laugh.

Chapter 21
Conclusion?

He sat there for a few moments, the assistants and the other two dentists staring at him in complete horror and shock. They had been standing there, staring at him the whole time. None of them had any clue of what to do. Eventually, they began to assume what might be happening before them but were left completely in the dark as to what was actually happening as he worked on the short and wide metal cylinder that looked to them like a fat coffee thermos.

Dr. Campbell then walked slowly and shakily out of the dental operatory to the back bathroom where he closed the door and began to scrub his face and his hands in the sink. He then took off his bloody and travel-worn clothes, trading them for one of the sets of dark blue scrubs in his size that were hanging on the rack.

He heard the sirens of the police, which he presumed had been contacted after he barged into the office covered with blood. Several officers with guns drawn entered the office and cautiously detained him and the remnants of the devices left in the dental operatory, escorting him out. He was cuffed and placed in one of the police cars. He had said nothing during the arrest, nothing of the bomb, nothing of the car he had sort of stolen from the raceway. His mind was mostly numb; his energy zapped from the constant adrenaline rush of the last hour, the last three days. He was escorted to the police station, where he was placed in a holding cell to wait for the interviewing officers.

He sat dazed on the bench and stared at a wall, reliving the last three days' adventures.

He was only in the holding cell for a little while as calls from various governmental agents and agencies had finally connected with the on-the-ground local law enforcement leadership to determine that he was not an accomplice but an unwilling participant who might have just prevented a terrorist attack.

What came next was a cheerful reuniting of husband and wife, father and children, coupled with long hours of story time—carefully curated and edited for the age and sensitivity level of his children. Intermingled with the recovery and family time was a lot of question-and-answer time and lots of discussions with law enforcement and CIA/FBI-type individuals.

No charges were filed, but there were still those who doubted that Dr. Campbell was really only incidentally and unintentionally in a photo with a known terrorist collaborator...

The End

Made in the USA
Monee, IL
11 November 2024